OF BOYS AND MEN

RENEE HARLESS

OF BOYS AND MEN

RENEE HARLESS

I had a past.
It was dark.
It was ugly.
It was my dirty secret.

No one knew the weight of the burdens that nearly
consumed me.
I lived with a singular focus—seeking revenge on my
father.

Then the new girl, Jolee Ward, moved into the apartment
above me and shattered my carefully constructed world.
We were like oil and water. . . until we weren't.
Then we detonated like gasoline and fire, but the inferno
threatened to destroy us both.
One night with her couldn't erase years spent plotting.

Wellington University wasn't big enough for the both of
us.

CHAPTER ONE

JOLEE

I did it.

I couldn't believe that I finally did it.

As the plane taxied down the runway to its final destination, I exhaled the deep breath I had been holding since the plane began its descent. The flight from Anchorage, Alaska to Boston, Massachusetts, was a long one, and through the entire trip, I couldn't help but recall how similarly my life matched that of Rapunzel's from the Disney movie, *Tangled*.

After living under my parents' strict watch for the last twenty years, I finally took the chance to go out on my own, despite their insistence and fear. I wanted to see what the world was like and what treasures it could hold for me. The day I received that acceptance letter to

Wellington Ridge University had been a game-changer. Miraculously I was given a few scholarships, which I desperately needed because my parents weren't going to help out one iota since I decided to transfer from the local college. The rest of the funds were coming from my savings and a job I found close to campus.

The only reason my parents didn't completely lose their sanity over my pleas to study somewhere else was that my cousin, Willow, attended the college where I would be transferring.

As the plane settled into place I shot a message to my cousin and let her know that I had landed, she had promised to meet me at baggage claim. A welcoming face to greet me was going to be worth the long flight. Thankfully, I didn't bring much with me; one checked bag, a carryon, and my laptop. Everything else was mailed or I planned to purchase it when I arrived.

Exiting the aircraft, I followed the masses toward baggage claim, where I found Willow standing nervously by the farthest corner, anxiously glancing at any person that walked passed her. She looked just as I remembered. Her long blonde hair, similar to mine but with tight, spiral curls, was pulled into a messy bun on the top of her head while she looked casual in a pair of jeans and a navy blue T-shirt.

Willow smiled a dimpled grin when she noticed me and I generously smiled in return. We'd only met in person three times, but as the cousins closest in age, we video chatted almost daily. She understood what this journey meant for me, how difficult it was for me to leave everything behind, but she encouraged me to stand up for myself and spread my wings. If I ever wanted out of the small town, I needed to do it soon.

"Did you have a good flight?" she asked in her soft voice.

"It wasn't what I expected," I told her as I rolled my carryon toward the conveyor with the rest of the passengers and waited for my one suitcase to make its way down the path. She followed along with me, her eyes darting around constantly.

"Are you okay?" I asked her wondering about her anxious nature.

"Sorry, I'm just not a huge fan of crowds." I nodded in understanding. Crowds weren't my favorite thing either; that's another reason I chose Wellington Ridge. The University was on the smaller side since it was a private college.

"Anyway, the flight was fine. I expected it to feel confining and scary, but once we hit altitude and people started moving around, I felt more comfortable."

I spotted my bright pink suitcase and gripped the handle before it passed, the heavy case landing with a thud as I yanked it down. The zippers were tightened to their max and I was worried that I'd find the contents inside draped along the conveyor, but so far, it seemed to be withstanding the pressure.

Together, Willow and I made our way out of the airport and waited in line for the shuttle that would take us back to the University. She had informed me that the shuttle is one of the luxuries provided by the upper-class private college – money made things happen. I didn't have money, not like Willow. All I had to my name was my meager savings from working as a veterinary assistant the last three years and the job waiting for me to start in a week.

Willow came into a healthy inheritance when her grandmother passed away when she was in high school – the same grandmother that left nothing to my family. Another point of contention my parents had with me deciding to move and be closer with that side of the family. We never discussed the falling out. I made the mistake of asking once and I learned never to ask again.

The shuttle ride lasted about an hour and my nose was glued to the window the entire time. I had never seen so many historic buildings or so much traffic.

Anchorage was busy, but it was nothing like this. And the suburban town my parents called home boasted no more than five thousand residents. I was in awe.

The prestigious gates of the school came into view and I felt like I had traveled back in time. The woodwork and stone seemed ancient amongst the bustling city, even though I knew from research that the school had been established in the 1950's, but it had always been a functioning college since it's construction in the late 1890's.

"Wow," I murmured as my gaze flicked back and forth across the expansive landscape. This was the place I was going to call home for the next two years. This was the place where I'd learn who I was, not who my parents wanted me to be.

"It's pretty, isn't it?" Willow asks as she chuckled at my expression.

"It's far better than I imagined, and we both know that I have quite the imagination," I pointed out, recalling the few stories I had concocted on video chats with Willow.

The shuttle stopped outside of the library and let us out, the driver helping me with my large suitcase as I stepped down onto the sidewalk. I smiled warmly at him in thanks and I was surprised when I got nothing more than a grunt in response.

With her hand gesturing around us, Willow exclaimed, "So, this is it. Are you ready?"

"Not in the slightest."

"You'll be fine, just keep to yourself and try to blend in. They'll leave you alone," she said as we started the trek to her, well now, our apartment.

"What did you mean about being left alone?" I asked, trying to maneuver the large suitcase while also taking in my surroundings. Willow trotted ahead with my carryon and laptop bag.

"I'm not sure how it is in Alaska, but this college has the same cliques that you'd find in high school, except there are fewer rules and more alcohol."

"Oh," I whispered. I remembered some of public high school, but I spent my junior and senior years in an online classroom graduating early.

"You're pretty, I'm sure you'll be fine," Willow made sure to point out, which left me wondering if she found herself on the wrong side of the mean girls. I always thought Willow had an understated beauty that no one could match.

We continued our walk through the campus until we reached the opposite end. Rows of homes and apartments spread out before me. Dark side was what Willow called the area and clarified that it was because they had fewer street lamps than light side, which was where fraternity and sorority row resided.

I followed her blindly, switching my hands on the suitcase handle as my arm began to tire. Finally, my cousin stopped at the front of a large apartment building. Christmas lights and tiki torches lined the balcony railings. Kegs were stacked in a pyramid near the dumpster in the parking lot. Music thumped from an apartment close by. And I had never felt so far out of my element before.

"This is. . ." My words lingered in the air. I couldn't quite describe what was laid out in front of me. I wasn't necessarily disappointed, but for some reason, I expected more.

Since I enrolled at the college with a bachelor's degree already under my wing and enough prerequisite credits from the local college to qualify me as a junior, I wasn't required to live in the college dorms. I lucked out that Willow had secured an apartment for herself and her two previous roommates, then one of them decided not to return to school. It seemed like everything had worked in my favor, up until now.

But my luck always seemed to have a way of running out when I needed it most.

"It gets better inside," Willow assured me, her skeptical eyes running over my fearful expression. "We have an apartment on the top floor with a great view of the nature reserve." She knew where my heart lay.

Nodding, I began to follow her up the stairs, one at a time, as I heaved the suitcase behind me. We had four flights to go. Willow stopped at the first landing to wait for me, and once I reached the top of the first flight, I told her to go ahead without me. I knew the apartment number and didn't want to keep her waiting.

"Are you sure?" she asked, the bridge of her nose wrinkling as she contemplated my decision.

"Yes, of course. You'll just be standing around waiting. I'll be up in a bit. It's totally fine, Willow."

It took her an extra second, but she turned on her heels and sped up the stairwell, leaving me with my wobbly legs and a suitcase that seemed to gain weight during the trip. I tried not to inhale deeply since the stairwell had an odd scent wafting through the air.

Five minutes later, I turned the corner as I approached the landing between the second and third floors. I hadn't quite made it to the top, but I had long since lost the feeling in my fingers. Resting the suitcase on a stair, I released my hold and shook out my hands. The tingling of the nerves was a bit painful, but I was glad to get the blood flowing again.

I stayed in the spot for another minute, catching my breath. Four flights didn't seem like a lot, especially when I was used to hiking the mountains behind our house in Alaska daily, but it seemed I wasn't built for stair climbs while pulling a fifty-pound weight.

Just above me a door slammed shut, and I exhaled deeply knowing that I needed to move my suitcase out of the way. My arms hadn't quite recovered, so I wasn't surprised to find them shaking as I gripped the handle.

Holy pigs in a blanket.

A man stood at the top of the stairs, phone pressed to his ear, and he was the most beautiful thing I had ever seen. Did all of the boys here look like they walked out of a Calvin Klein ad?

I watched in rapture as he wound his fingers through his unruly dark hair and began his descent down the stairs.

Remembering that I blocked his way, I mustered up as much strength as I could, and I yanked on the handle once, then twice, in the hopes that the luggage would move out of his way. On the third tug, I realized my good luck had taken a nosedive.

The handle gripped tightly in my hand detached from the outer shell and I flew backward just as the man passed me while the case bounced back down the stairs. I barely had time to shout for him to watch out before the luggage clipped his leg just as my back slammed against the concrete stair behind me.

He gripped the handrail and turned his steely gaze toward me, ice practically shooting from his eyes.

"What the fuck?" the man snarled just as my suitcase landed with a thud on the bottom step.

That zipper I had been worried about? Well, it finally had enough and tore apart, releasing the contents inside. I'd never been more grateful to have picked up storage cubes, but my gratefulness didn't last long when the man kicked my suitcase and continued on his way, not giving me another glance.

Despite the pain in my back, which would inevitably turn into a hideous bruise, I gripped the rail and pulled myself up to lean over the side of the stairs.

"Thanks for the help, you. . . you. . .jerk." Name-calling wasn't my forte. I was taught to never curse, so I had to get creative, but he left me so flustered that I couldn't come up with anything interesting.

In response, he flipped his middle finger in the air. I knew what that gesture stood for.

How dare he?

My anger seethed. When was the last time someone treated me so carelessly? I could remember only once, and that did nothing to extinguish the fire igniting deep in my gut.

"Yeah? Well, I hope your momma knows that she raised no gentleman," I shouted, ignoring another door slamming above me.

That seemed to get his attention.

He turned his face back toward me, his nose flaring with every breath. God, he truly was quite the specimen, but apparently, I'd pissed him off. Well, served him right.

"Sorry," another man said as he scooted around me, his brown hair pulled back in a neat bun. He winced at my open suitcase and turned his eyes back toward me, regret filling them, then looked around the corner at the man who had focused his furious stare on me.

"J, do you need some help?" Willow called down from the top landing. I glanced up through a sliver in the stairwell, breaking my contact with Iceman.

"Yeah," I sighed. After the mess that was made, I was definitely going to need some help.

Turning back around, I found that the two men were long gone. What a great impression I've made on my new neighbors.

As Willow clambered down the steps, I made my way down to my suitcase, my back protesting as I bent forward to reorganize the mess and stuff it back inside. Except as Willow made it to the landing, I noticed that the zipper had completely torn away from the suitcase.

"Great," I grumbled, looking up at Willow as she nibbled at her lower lip. We huffed out a sigh simultaneously and reached down to grab a stack of the storage cubes.

"This is not how I wanted to start things off," I complained as I meticulously stacked the remainder of the cubes in my arms, blocking my line of sight.

Slowly, I followed Willow up the stairs and down the hallway until I watched her feet stop outside of an apartment door.

"This is us. Welcome home, Jolee."

Willow balanced her stack of cubes precariously in her arms as she opened the door. A minute later, I felt hands grip one of the piles in my arms and remove them, carrying them further into the apartment as I stood still in the hallway. Finally, the other stack was pulled from my grip and taken in to the apartment.

Inside, I was met with a small hallway, just wide enough for one person to pass through at a time. The wall to my left had a set of bi-fold doors that Willow described as a coat closet and a laundry area. We were lucky to have laundry in the space; I was not a fan of laundromats.

Slipping passed me, Willow explained that she was going to grab my broken suitcase while I looked around the apartment.

I barely made it through the entrance before a woman with jet black hair bumped into me, her glasses slipped down the bridge of her nose.

"Oh, I'm sorry," she squeaked.

"It's my fault. I wasn't looking where I was going."

She stared blankly at me as she removed her glasses from her face and wiped the lenses on her shirt. I didn't realize that purple eyes were real, and I absolutely would have thought this woman wore contacts if I hadn't noticed her extremely thick glasses, but she had the most stunning eye color I had ever seen. I couldn't stop staring.

"What?" she asked as she propped her glasses back on her face.

Ashamed to have been caught looking too long, I shook my head in embarrassment. This was not how I wanted to make a first impression. First, with the boy on the stairs and now with the girl that I assume will be my roommate.

"Nothing, I didn't mean to stare. It's just, you have beautiful eyes." My cheeks reddened in embarrassment. I couldn't believe I had admitted to her that I had been staring. "I'm sorry, that was incredibly rude of me."

Just as the awkward silence grew between us, Willow came gliding into the apartment with my broken suitcase.

"Oh, good. I'm glad we're all here," my ordinarily shy cousin said. "J, this is our roommate, Haley. She and I were suitemates in the dorms last year. Haley, this is my cousin, Jolee."

"Nice to meet you," I replied with my hand extended toward Haley. Thankfully she quickly shook my hand and smiled. And I could see that my momentary lapse of normalcy was easily dismissed.

After the introduction, I took in the living room, pleased to find it spacious and warm. The couch looked new and it faced a large television propped on top of a media cabinet, only a wooden coffee table separated the two items.

"The living room is great."

"Thanks," Willow replied. "But be careful with the coffee table, one of the legs wobbles."

Nodding, I turned around, taking in the kitchen. It was small and tight, but I didn't need a lot of room to cook. Willow made sure to show me my dedicated shelves in the refrigerator and the pantry, making sure that I knew what items were available for sharing like milk, butter, and eggs. The kitchen was exactly like she had told me on the phone, but I didn't bother pointing that out.

Following the girls down the hall where Haley and I had collided, Willow pointed out each of their rooms and then led me to the very last door. I placed my hand on the knob and turned the cold metal while holding my breath. This was the first time I would be living in a space that wasn't under my parents' reign. Even though I was twenty-two, I felt eighteen all over again.

The door slid across the tan carpet and I exhaled with a whoosh. The room wasn't massive, just big enough for a queen-sized bed, a dresser, a desk, and a nightstand, but the knot in my chest tightened. This space was mine. It would be the place I would make my dreams a reality. It would be my home.

Willow began to speak from behind me, but the heartbeat pounding in my ears drowned her out. Spinning on my heels, I grabbed my cousin in a tight embrace and squeezed her as if she were going to drift away. This woman had offered me a sanctuary in a time that I needed it most, and I would be eternally grateful. Nothing could mess this up for me, this opportunity to live my own life.

I released her just as quickly and stepped into my bedroom, turning around as I took it all in. There was a large picture window facing the reserve's park across the street and I imagined the afternoons I would spend beneath its sills watching the world come alive.

"Where did the furniture come from?" I inquired as I ran my hand over the gray dresser. The wood was solid and warm beneath my touch, and I knew that not only was it beautiful – it was expensive. There was a wrought-iron bed across from me with a nightstand that matched the dresser. It was exactly what I would have chosen for myself.

When I didn't get an immediate response, I turned away from the window and stared at Willow, who was twisting her fingers together in front of her body. Haley took a leisurely step backward.

I knew the answer then. I knew that somehow, Willow had done this for me.

"Willow, I. . ." I began.

"J, I knew that you didn't have a lot of money to splurge on furniture. So I told Mother that I needed a new bedroom set. She didn't even blink an eye. I picked out the furniture with Haley over the summer. Are you mad?"

Willow worried her lip, scared of my reaction, and it took all of my strength not to shed the tears welling in my eyes.

"Thank you. It's. . .it's perfect. It's exactly what I would have chosen."

Her worried expression quickly morphed into relief. Had she really been worried that I would be ungrateful or angry at her selfless gesture?

The girls helped me carry the storage cubes into my bedroom and I put away what I could. There was only one bathroom for the three of us, which I wasn't so sure was going to be the easiest situation when getting ready for classes and work, but I wasn't going to be choosy.

Willow and Haley offered to show me around campus so that I was ready for classes on Monday and I eagerly accepted their gesture. I needed just a few minutes to take a quick shower and change my clothes. My skin felt dry and scratchy from the recycled air of the plane and I yearned to wash it away.

The water was heavenly and when I stepped out of the bathroom after a quick rinse, I felt new and refreshed. Looking at the few clothes I had brought with me, my excitement quickly diminished. There wasn't enough research in the world to tell me what to expect when I arrived here. At the college I previously attended, the majority of my classmates showed up in either pajamas or loungewear. I was confident that a prestigious university outside of Boston would require a more upper-class appearance, which was why I had packed a few dressy shorts in various colors, classy shirts, and a pale pink sheath dress. Judging by Willow and Haley's appearances earlier, I had chosen incorrectly.

The only casual items I had with me were the jeans that I had worn on the plane and my green T-shirt, neither of which I had any desire to put over my clean body again.

Begrudgingly I slipped on a pair of white shorts and a blue lace camisole, thankful that Boston's temperature wasn't too dissimilar from Anchorage's. I was going to have to deal with my wardrobe for now until I got a few more paychecks under my belt. Clothes were not a necessary expense.

Winding my hair into a neat knot on the top of my head and slipping my feet into a pair of fake leather sandals, I walked toward the living room where my cousin and Haley were waiting for me.

Both girls blinked up at me from the couch when I entered the room and I could immediately sense that they wanted to say something.

"I know. I made a bad choice with clothes, but all I had at home were my scrubs for work and the jeans I wore on the plane."

Rising up from the couch, Willow circled around me. "Did you raid my mother's closet?"

"I can't afford anything else until I get my first paycheck," I retorted. Looking over to Haley, I asked, "Am I going to stand out?"

"Oh, you're definitely going to stand out," she explained, and then added, "but it won't be because of your clothes."

I didn't have time to question her comment as Willow dragged Haley and me from the apartment. Our feet ate up the pavement as we walked toward campus, the buildings aged before my eyes, but not in a bad way.

The structures changed from wood to brick, then brick to stone. It was magnificent to take in.

My heart sped up as we walked down alleyways between the buildings. Willow made sure to point out which buildings held my classes. I almost got the hang of the school's octagonal layout when the growling of my stomach echoed across the fountain. If I hadn't stood out before, I certainly did then as a few classmates looked up from their perches on the grass.

It wasn't my fault; I hadn't eaten since the day before and the time change had severely messed with my schedule.

Willow and Haley slunk away from me, obviously attempting not to draw attention to themselves. Still, as the gathering around us continued to stare in my direction, their eyes darted to my roommates.

"Sorry," I mumbled, noticing how much I truly stood out amongst the masses. The guys mostly wore gym shorts and T-shirts, but the girls were on an entirely new level. They were either dressed for a night of partying at a club like I had seen in the movies, or wore denim shorts cut and frayed to show as much leg as possible with midriff-baring tops.

I had never felt out of shape; more or less, I always thought that I was average-sized, but compared to the women lying across blankets on the school lawn, I would never measure up. These women looked as if they walked right off the runway with their perfectly blown-out hair and perfect bodies.

As Willow directed me away from the center of the school, I could feel everyone's eyes still latched onto me. Maybe it was a mistake for me to transfer to such a small school. I was beginning to regret my decision.

"You'll love the cheesy tater tots at Joe's," Willow said as we continued to follow her out of the quad.

Haley startled us when she screeched, "Oh gosh," and tucked her chin to her chest, covering her face with her dark hair.

"What is it?" I asked, craning my neck to look around, wondering what had frightened her. But as my eyes land on movement to my left, I had to reach out for Haley's arm as I tripped on my own feet.

"The rogues," Willow whispered, mimicking Haley's movement by using her hair to cover her face.

"The what?" I inquired as I regained my balance and stared directly at the grouping of six men.

"Don't look at them!" Willow admonished as she tugged at my arm urging me to continue walking, but I found myself pinned in place. Not by my feet, but by the angered gaze locked on me by one of them. "The ridge rogues. That's what everyone at Wellington University calls them. The gorgeous bad boys that every girl wants to claim and every guy wants to be."

A huff of laughter bubbled from my throat as I turned away from his steely gaze to look at Willow. "That's not a thing," I told her.

"Oh, it most certainly is a thing. You do not want to be on the rogue's bad side, because if they don't like you, no one is going to like you. Come on."

I didn't dare tell them that I had already experienced my first run-in with the rogues. To be honest, I wasn't even sure if Haley and Willow knew that the bad boys lived on the floor below us. All I knew was if what they said was true, then I already had a slew of enemies against me because I could feel the fury filled stare of one particular rogue the entire time that I walked away.

CHAPTER TWO

FORD

I prided myself on being even-keeled the majority of the time. My temper didn't flare often. Of course, that could be due to the surly expression I wore on my face. I had very little to be happy about.

Frustration already fueled me by the time the gorgeous, but vile woman struck me with her suitcase. I'm not sure what her expectations were, because I certainly hadn't dropped and broken her luggage, but she gave me a look of hatred. One that I made sure to return as well, especially after she launched her scathing words in my direction.

No, my mother sure didn't raise a gentleman. She never got the chance to raise me at all. Hearing her say those words ignited an anger in me that I solely left burning for my sperm donor.

No amount of her beauty could make up for the ugliness that girl festered in me.

My brother of sorts, Link, mumbled a few choice words at me as we left the apartment and headed onto campus. We were meeting the rest of our adoptive brothers outside the Arts building to help Tracy move her office.

Tracy was our adoptive mother. I had never met a woman more deserving of sainthood than her. She and Adam, her husband, took in six boys and raised us as her own. My cousin, Tyler, and I came to her when we were each around preschool age when the state took us in, but Link, Archer, Chance, and Rylan all came when they were older. It took a brave family to take on that many boys, especially the ones known to cause trouble.

But five years ago, our adoptive father died from a heart attack. It had been hard on all of us, but Tracy never wavered with her love. So when she called asking for help to switch her office to a new location, I knew that everyone would show up.

When we arrived outside the building, the rest of my brothers were waiting with a gathering of women vying for their attention, even Tyler, who was still in high school.

Women were willing to do just about anything to say that they had bagged a rogue. We knew what our classmates called us – the ridge rogues, the bad boys of Wellington University, even though the ones of us that attended the college did so on scholarships and honors. Our intellect didn't matter to them; they saw us as the handsome, leather-wearing men of their fantasies. But as a few of the women turned their attention toward me, I couldn't say that I minded being the star of their fantasies. So long as they knew my rules.

No repeats.

No kisses.

And absolutely no love.

I had too much on my plate to get caught up in a relationship, too much at stake to risk turning off my path.

From beside me, I watched as Archer ran his hands through his hair, his dark locks skimmed his eyes, and the women gathered around him swooned. Their sighs of pleasure at watching him move was almost sickening. He was their god and could command them to do anything he wanted.

"Tell your girls to scram," I commanded as I jabbed my elbow into his ribs.

They scattered apart after Archer grunted at them to go away.

"Where's Tracy?" I asked Tyler, who would have ridden with her.

"She was finishing up a phone call in the car."

Nodding, I shoved my hands in my jean pockets and leaned against the brick railing of the steps. There were a lot of students out on the lawn enjoying the warm weather before classes started on Monday, but I had little desire to be amongst them. A gathering of any kind wasn't something that I enjoyed; I never knew if someone had ulterior motives.

"Well, well, well," Archer cat-called as a trio of women walked by. I swore under my breath. That man thought with his dick more than his brain sometimes, even though he was a certified genius.

I craned my neck to steal a glance at whatever had captured his attention. Unbridled need instantly washed over me as I took in the woman's long legs.

Damn, what I wouldn't give "to feel those beauties wrapped around my waist," Archer completed my thought aloud.

All of the boys leaned closer to get a better look as the three women crossed the pathway in front of the fountain. I noticed that they'd not only garnered our attention, but the men and women lounging on the lawn couldn't take their eyes off them either.

"Isn't that. . .?" Link let his question linger in the air until my attention traveled up to their faces. Two of the girls I recognized from campus, but it wasn't until the other female turned around that I realized I knew who she was all along.

She was gorgeous, there was no question of that, and my cock instantly jerked behind my jeans in awareness. But my groan was not one of pleasure; it was one of disgust.

"That's the girl from the stairs," I concluded for him.

My eyes never moved from their lock on her - I couldn't pull them away if I tried. She was all that I could see, a vignette focused around her body. And I hated it.

"You know her?" Archer asked before my other brothers began peppering their own questions.

I couldn't hear them over the buzzing in my ear. God, just looking at the woman infuriated me. Not only had she pissed me off barely an hour ago, but she made me lose my train of thought.

Our eyes latched and held as she looked over her shoulder at us, her friends obviously whispering warnings to her. Something about the way she measured me with her gaze made me feel as if she found me lacking. Me? I could have any woman at this school with the snap of my finger and she looked at me with disdain. Like I was no more than a leech or cockroach to her.

Well, fuck her and her preppy self. I didn't even care that the sun gleamed off her shiny blonde hair, or that despite her petite body, her legs seemed to go on for miles. I was fairly certain she was wearing a shirt that Tracy had hanging in her closet. None of her beauty could detract from the way she irritated me with a single glance.

Turning toward my brothers, I looked at them harshly. I could sense their interest in her and her two friends, their eyes tracked each of the women's movements.

"No," I declared as I pushed away from the railing. "Stay away from her. She's a distraction none of us needs right now."

Cocking an eyebrow at me, a move that certainly had a few women clambering for him, Link silently begged me for more information. He wasn't getting any.

"Don't go all professor on me," I told him as I began to make my way up the building stairs knowing my brothers would follow. "There isn't any more to the story other than I can tell that she doesn't belong here. I mean, did you look at her?"

"Oh boy, did I," Archer groaned, and I had to fight back the urge to pound my fist into his face. Not only would I have a slew of angry females chasing after me for turning their god's face black and blue, but Tracy and my brothers would be upset. And I never wanted to do anything to hurt her or this family.

"So, what do you know about them?" Chance asked.

"Nothing," I mumbled as I opened the door to the building, deciding that waiting inside was a better option than the humid heat of Boston in August. But at the same time, Link added, "They live on the floor above us."

I didn't wait to hear the guys cheer knowing that attractive females were living in our building. Hell, there were beautiful females everywhere on campus. That was one of the best things about Wellington University.

The quietest of my brothers followed closely behind me. His heavy footsteps pounded against the floor.

"What did she do to piss you off already?" he asked, his question lingering in the air. "Ford."

"Nothing. Okay?"

My brother annoyingly grabbed my arm and twisted me to face him. Rylan never left questions hanging. He didn't speak much, preferring to showcase his vocal prowess with music, but when he spoke, you listened. Or like right now, if he asked you a question, you better be prepared to answer.

"Ford, you don't get worked up over anything. Out of all of us, you're the most even-keeled, probably because you have so much anger bundled up inside you directed toward your birth father. So, forgive me if seeing a rise out of you over a female has me questioning why."

It was the most I had heard him speak in years, but damn if he was anything but observant. My entire life revolved around the pent up rage that I had toward my sperm donor. There was absolutely nothing to extinguish it, nothing to temper the flame - until her. She diverted my attention – even if for a split second. My thoughts were drawn away from the man that destroyed my life and focused on a woman with a stupid piece of luggage. Her large brown eyes questioned why I didn't help her, why I kept walking past even though her broken suitcase knocked my leg and sprawled its contents on the ground.

I was willing to ignore it all until she brought up my mother and how she raised me. *That* had been too much. *That* had been the ice to freeze me in place and stare back at her, wanting so badly to simultaneously rip off her clothes and rip out her heart.

No one. Not a single person had that effect on me.

But I couldn't tell that to Rylan or my brothers. They'd instantly sprout off more questions. Questions that I didn't have the answers to.

"Look, I don't know her at all. But I had the pleasure of running over her on the stairwell when her suitcase fell, knocking me on the back of my leg and almost tripping me," I explained to Rylan, who immediately asked if she was okay, and I vaguely recollected her falling backward, the concrete stairs colliding with her hips and spine. But she seemed fine when she shouted back at me. When Link joined me we left without a backward glance.

"She's fine."

"Hmm. . ." he mumbled as we approached Tracy's old office, our brothers not far behind.

I could see Link and Archer silently wanted to know more about the new woman, while Tyler looked busy on his phone. Thank goodness for the tall woman with the graying hair approaching, a wide smile on her face as she took us all in.

Tracy was our savior through and through. Not many families wanted to adopt older boys – troubled ones at that. Hell, Chance had already been to juvenile detention twice by the time he was ten. The state begged Tracy to take him in, and she had with open arms. Once he knew that she wasn't going to send him away, he changed his attitude, just as we all had.

"How are my boys?" she asked us as if we hadn't all gathered for dinner the night before.

We mumbled our responses in unison as she opened her office door. There were boxes filled to the brim with her books and office equipment, but the rest of the space was empty.

"Thanks for helping. I just have a few things remaining."

"Why are you moving?" I asked as I lifted the box closest to me, silently thankful that it didn't weigh more than it looked.

Tracy smiled and I couldn't help but return the gesture. "I was offered one on the upper floor. A corner office with two walls of windows."

Now I understood why she was excited. Tracy had loved the outdoors, and growing up, she and Adam had taken us hiking on the weekends, fishing in the summer, and sledding in the winter. If it wasn't raining, we were all outside.

"Can't wait to see it," I told her as I stepped toward the doorway where she stood. Tracy gently rested her hand on my cheek and the motion reminded me of all the times as a young boy she would do the same. Always telling me that I was worthy of love. Somehow she knew when my anger had festered into a place that would eat me alive. That gentle touch of hers always calmed me, as if she could take my anger into herself and give me a few moments of peace.

In all these years, that feeling never changed, never faltered. The touch calmed us all, each of her boys fighting our own internal demons, each of us feeling fury and rage toward the circumstances that brought us to our savior. It was hard not to after what we had each gone through.

Her gaze skimmed over me, searching wordlessly for the cause of my anger. But instead of an inquisition, I was met with a smile, a smile tilting upward on the corner of her lips.

"Are you going to see your mother today?" she asked as she gently patted my cheek then released her touch.

Tucking my chin toward my chest, I whispered, "Yes." I hated knowing that I may cause an ounce of pain for Tracy whenever I went to see my biological mother. But if it ever hurt her, she never let on. If anything, Tracy always encouraged me to visit my mother. She knew the circumstances surrounding my relationship with my birth parents.

"Good. Please tell her I said hello."

"Yes, ma'am."

With each of us carrying a box, we followed Tracy down the hall to the elevator, the heads of students and teachers popping out of the rooms and offices to take a look at us. We always drew a crowd no matter where we were.

It took two trips to get everything to Tracy's new office and then another hour to set it up the way that she wanted. All six of us humbly watched as Tracy placed a framed picture on the top tier of her bookshelf. It was taken on our last hiking trip before Adam had his heart attack. We were all standing together, a waterfall off in the distance, and a lake beneath our feet. Adam had his arm lovingly wrapped around Tracy's shoulders, and not two seconds later, he had tossed her into the chilled water. We all followed suit, then regretted it during the hike back, but no one's smile had been brighter than theirs. We weren't the traditional family, but love and happiness oozed from our makeshift parents in spades.

From the other side of the desk, I watched as Tracy took her time admiring the picture, tilting the frame until the light from her window shone on it just right. I had lost a lot in my life, and losing Adam had been hard, but I couldn't imagine losing the love of my life the way Tracy had. They were what couples aspired to be.

"Mom," I called out, choking on the word as it fell from my lips. I didn't use the endearment often, and Tracy understood why, but at this moment, it seemed right. Her shoulders moved up as she took a deep breath, then she released them as she turned, a false smile plastered on her face. Using the side of her hand, she wiped away a lone tear as Link stepped forward and wrapped his arm around her shoulder. We could feel her sorrow still rampant at her loss, though she masked it well.

"Sorry 'bout that, boys." She should know that she never needed to apologize for missing her husband, we all felt the same, not enough years had passed, and I doubt I would feel differently ten or twenty years from now. "How about we go get some pizza?"

The sadness in the room dissipated as agreements and cheers went around. I felt terrible for bailing, and I could tell that Tracy noticed, but she didn't let on as we followed her out of the building toward the parking lot.

I stood by the black '67 Camaro Adam had helped me restore in high school, watching as the guys headed toward their own vehicles. Tracy stopped beside me.

"Have a good time with your mother, Ford."

"Thanks," I replied. There wasn't a proper response to give regarding my visits with my mother. I only ever left more confused and angry.

"I can see that something is weighing on your mind and I hope you know that I'm always here to listen."

That feeling of someone being able to read me always made me uncomfortable. My hand automatically went to the back of my neck, rubbing my skin and overgrown hair.

"Tracy, I. . ." I wanted to get it off my chest. To confess everything that had been dragging me down these last few months and was eating away at me. But I wasn't ready and I didn't think she was either.

I drew my eyes away from my mom and noticed something white from the corner of my eye. The girl from the stairwell was making her way back to the apartment

with her two friends, her blonde hair now wrapped in a
messy knot on the top of her head, showcasing her
slender neck. My eye was drawn to those damn white
shorts that should have done nothing for her small body
but cupped a perfectly round ass. I hated that she was
pulling my attention away from something important –
again.

My eyes lingered too long, and my jaw ticked as I
tried to fight against what I was feeling at that moment. I
was certain Tracy could tell that something had captured
my attention. I didn't move my gaze away fast enough.

Instead of asking questions or prying, Tracy did
what she did best, she patted the side of my cheek and
told me that she loved me, then headed toward her car
where Tyler waited.

With my hip leaned against the side of my car, I
lingered in the parking lot as I watched everyone drive
away. My mom was waiting for our weekly meeting, but
I wasn't quite ready to head out yet, it always took a toll
on me. Not just emotionally, but mentally. It took hours
after my visits for me to unwind after seeing her, the
thread holding onto my sanity twisting until it began
shredding from the pressure.

I drove to my mom's place, the car eating up the
miles until I turned onto the flower-lined path kept

pristine by a gardener. It was like makeup, made to look beautiful on the outside to hide the ugly beyond its gates.

I parked the car in my usual spot and made my way through the door, where an unfamiliar face greeted me.

"Hello, sir. Can I help you?" the burly man asked as I continued to walk down the hall, ignoring his question. "Sir! I can't let you back there."

Without glancing over my shoulder, I shouted, "Ask anyone here, they know who I am."

Finally, I stopped at the door painted pale pink, and felt the corner of my mouth tilt upward in a smile. Knocking once, I turned the knob and entered the room.

The setting sun beamed through the large pane window, washing the room in oranges and pinks – her favorite colors. Flowers were spread out on every surface, masking the smell of bleach and death.

"Rutherford, is that you?" the dark-haired woman called out from her reading chair in the corner. I vowed that I would get her out of this place and I worked harder every day to make that happen. I was almost there and the tips of my fingers brushed the surface just outside my grasp.

Soon.

"Hey, Mom."

CHAPTER THREE

JOLEE

Today was the day.

I had woken up an hour before my alarm was scheduled to ring, which had me bright-eyed and bushy-tailed at the ungodly hour of 5 a.m. I usually wasn't a morning person, but the first day of school always excited me. Learning was one of my favorite things, the way it opened up your mind as you fed yourself new information about the world surrounding you taught me more about myself than anything.

The coffee maker brewed my second cup as I skimmed through my cabinet for something to eat for breakfast. My first class was at nine, so I had plenty of time to get ready.

"Good morning," I called out to Willow as she shuffled into the kitchen. Her answering response was a heavy grunt. When she stole my cup of coffee, I didn't reprimand her; I silently brewed another cup.

She sighed into her cup as she took her first gulp, closing her eyes as the caffeine swam through her system.

"How are you so awake this morning, and what are you wearing?" she asked just as Haley ventured out of her room. We all had our first classes of the semester at 9 a.m.

"I've been up for a few hours," I mumbled as I looked down at my pink sheath dress. Despite it being far from casual, I actually liked it. It made me feel more grown-up.

From behind me, I heard Haley say, "I can loan you a shirt and shorts if you want."

Was it really that bad? I didn't think so.

The girls must have sensed my uneasiness as I peered down at my clothes, wiping my hands down the material.

"That's okay. I'll make due until I get my first paycheck."

"You start your job this afternoon, right?" Willow asked as she grabbed a box of marshmallow cereal and a bowl from the cabinet.

"Yep. Thank goodness I can walk there."

I was lucky to find a veterinary office about three blocks from the university that needed extra help. I loved animals and had three years as a veterinary technician assistant under my belt and I was grateful to have the chance to continue growing my experience.

"Do you know if the animal shelter is close by?" I questioned as I filled my second cup of coffee.

"We aren't allowed pets unless we pay the fee," Haley grumbled behind her banana.

"Oh, I know. I just like to volunteer."

They both nodded, finished their breakfasts, and made their way to their bedrooms to get ready for class, leaving me to flip through the television channels while I waited. Casually I propped my foot up on the coffee table, only to have it wobble under the weight.

"Going to have to remember that," I surmised as I put my foot back on the floor and slumped against the cushions to watch the news.

It wasn't too long later that my roommates appeared and together we left the apartment. My steps slightly faltered as I reached the landing for the third floor. I wondered if I was going to run into him again, or if I'd see him around campus – the man with the icy gaze. He had an air about him and was probably used to getting whatever he wanted. But despite my irritation with him, he'd been all I could think about since our altercation last Thursday.

"J, you comin'?" Willow called out, waiting for me on the next landing. I rushed down the steps, promising that I wouldn't glance back up at the third floor, but my curiosity got the better of me, and I found myself peering over my shoulder one last time before it was entirely out of view.

The campus and walkways were empty except for a few early students like us. I had always figured that a 9 a.m. class would be more popular than an 8 a.m., but Willow informed me that the school conformed its scheduling to accommodate afternoon classes. It seemed strange to me, but I supposed that if you're a private college, you can do what you want. That notion seemed to seep down to its students as well.

Haley and Willow went their separate ways, both wishing me luck. They knew that my nerves were strung high today. I didn't do well with change and uncertainty. It took an entire year at the last college for me to feel comfortable there.

The steps to the economics and business building felt like sludging through thick mud I was so nervous, and once I reached the stairs leading inside, I faltered.

Could I do this?

I already had a degree, one that would serve me well for what I planned to do with my life, but I knew a business master's degree would help. I just needed to get the prerequisites out of the way.

Taking the first step, I mumbled to myself to be strong and that it was just an entry-level economics class. My body felt lighter when I reached the top and I was surprised to find more people milling about inside the entryway. But just like Thursday, their eyes were pinned on me. I felt like I was trapped inside a glass tank. My cheeks reddened as someone new entered the building, knocking my shoulder in the process. I wasn't sure how long I had been standing there, but it must have been too long to be necessary.

Scurrying through the doors into the hallway, I kept my head down as I breezed past the students still gawking at me. I was mortified, and as my eyes landed on my pink dress, I was even more embarrassed. Standing out wasn't what I had ever wanted, much preferring to stand along the sidelines while someone else's star shone brightly. And here I was, drawing the attention of everyone with my clothes and mini-panic attack. I regretted not accepting Haley's offer to borrow some clothes until I could afford new ones. Even more so,

I hated that I spent money on the ones I did bring, hoping to blend in.

Short, shallow breaths filled my lungs as I tried to calm myself. I knew there was no reason to get worked up, school was what was important any way, not what these privileged kids thought of me.

Just as I reached the stairwell that would take me to the third floor, I smacked into a wall of muscles. As I apologized, my eyes traveled up the neatly pressed white button-up shirt to a pair of kind eyes. They belonged to the second man in the apartment hall, the one with his hair still tied back behind his head.

"Are you okay?" he asked gently and I found myself intrigued by the roughness of his voice.

"Yes, um. . .I'm sorry, I wasn't looking where I was going."

More eyes pinned to me as passersby took in the interaction. Their gazes were silent, but to me, they were deafening.

"Do you need any help finding your way?" he asked, just as the alarm sounded on my phone, signaling that there was ten minutes before my class would start.

Taking two giant steps back, I shook my head and told him that I could find my class, then waved as I joined the other students heading up the stairs.

Everyone kept a wide berth from me, the distance growing with each step that I took, until the space felt suffocating. My blood was pumping double-time, not from the exertion, but mortification, and I wanted nothing more than to rush back down the stairs and back to the apartment. It would be easier to allow my dream to die, to change my focus to something else, but I knew how empty I'd feel if I let it go.

Finally, I reached the door that led to the classroom. Peering through the rectangular glass cutout, I realized that the chairs were empty. For the first time this morning, a smile grew on my lips as I opened the door and headed toward my favorite seat. The auditorium style seating was parted down the middle and I took that pathway to the second seat in the second row. Not too close, and not on the end. I also had a thing for the number two.

Rifling through my bag, I pulled out my beat-up laptop and opened the dictation program that I liked to use, even though I knew most of this first class would be used for discussing the syllabus.

It wasn't long before the rest of the room filled, but I noticed that, just like the stairwell, there was a wide berth of space around me. Not a single person sat in the row before me or the two rows behind, yet they filled the rows on the other half of the room. Panic oozed through my nerves that maybe there was something wrong with me, but I had made sure that both my hair and makeup looked nice when I left the apartment. And despite my dress, everyone else looked somewhat put together.

Grabbing my phone, I shot a text to Haley and Willow in our group chat.

Me: This is a nightmare.

Willow: Hang in there!

Haley: It will get better. Maybe you'll meet a cute guy!

A chuckle sounded in my chest as I put my phone away. Leave it to Haley to make me laugh with the thoughts of a guy. Men and relationships were the farthest things from my mind.

When I settled back in my seat, two girls entered the room, their gazes flickering back and forth across the uneven seating before looking at each other again. I could instantly tell that they were new to the school and just as confused as me.

A weight that I didn't realize was pressing against my chest lifted as they headed down my row and sat next to me. I smiled and suppressed the urge to jump up and cheer when they both returned a warm grin.

"Hi, I'm Keeley and this is my roommate, Sarah. We just transferred here," the girl next to me said as she pulled out her laptop from her bag.

"Same! It's like an entirely different world here at Wellington," I replied, and simultaneously the three of us peered around the room, taking it all in. "I'm Jolee, by the way."

"Oh, I love your name," Sarah claimed as she peered around Keeley.

The three of us may be outcasts, but we could be outcasts together. Of course, I'd hate if they were automatically placed in that category just for sitting with me and acknowledging my presence. But for some reason, both girls didn't seem like they would care.

The professor chose that moment to walk in and settle his bag on the large desk at the front of the room. Glancing at the clock on my laptop, I realized that we only had three minutes before the class would begin. Willow had taken this class last semester. She told me the professor was a stickler for punctuality and he would lock the door the second class was to start.

With one minute to spare, the students turned in unison as the door to the room opened. Women squealed with delight at the entrance, but I found myself suppressing a groan. It was the boy from the apartment. Ford, Willow had informed me was his name. Turning my gaze away from him, I pecked at my laptop to start the dictation program. I'd hoped that he'd ignore me and find a seat with the minions he had calling for him across the way.

"You're in my seat," he growled, his breath tickling my ear as he leaned into my space. I felt his shadow looming over me, instantly cooling my skin and sending a shiver down my spine. Of course, I couldn't be so lucky to have him overlook me.

Keeley squeaked in her seat beside me, and though I knew the students were whispering about Ford and me, I couldn't make out any noises beyond the heavy breathing coming from the man bent over the open seat.

Turning my gaze up to him, I made sure to harden my expression even though I wanted to take my time memorizing his face. He really was a beautiful man, more than I had first thought.

"This isn't your seat."

He looked taken aback by my comment, narrowing his eyes at the thought that I doubted what he said. And confused that I would question him.

"I always sit in this seat during my classes," he tried to explain, but to my ear, he sounded like a petulant child whining about a toy he couldn't have.

"Well, you're going to have to find a new one because I'm not moving." His jaw ticked as he stood up, and I knew that I shouldn't find the move sexy, but I did. And the way he narrowed his eyes at me, I almost wanted to see how many more buttons of his I could push.

"Take a seat, Mr. O'Brien," the professor called out as he locked the entrance door.

Refusing to acknowledge him further, and secretly hoping he'd slink away to one of the women calling for him, I kept my attention to the front of the classroom. My skin grew hot under everyone's watchful eye and I felt my cheeks flame, the blush of my pale skin matching that of my dress. I was about to slump farther down in my seat until I felt a kick at the back of my chair. Turning swiftly, I locked gazes with Ford as he settled into the seat directly behind me.

"You're a jerk," I seethed, my hand clenching the back of my seat until the knuckles turned white. He only fostered more annoyance as he casually draped his arm across the chair beside him and settled one of his boot-clad feet on his ripped black denim. All while a casual smirk rested on his full lips.

It was as I began to turn back around that I noticed how quiet the room had grown and that everyone, including the professor, had their attention on me.

"Do you have something to say, Ms. . .?" the professor asked.

"Ward," I added. "Jolee Ward. And no, sir."

"Great, let's get started," he said sarcastically as he turned toward the screen displaying the syllabus.

As the professor's back was turned, I glanced back at Ford once more, a notebook and pen casually placed on the small desk attached to Ford's chair. He winked in my direction and I promised myself that it was the last time I'd give him my attention.

And it took everything during the class to keep that promise, especially when the professor stated that we had to remain in these seats the rest of the year. Keeley, Sarah, and I exchanged subtle smiles at the proclamation, only to have Ford "accidentally" knock the back of my chair again.

Jerk.

By the end of the hour and a half discussion, I was exhausted. Not because of boredom or the introduction to the economics course, but because I had been on pins and needles the entire time. I kept waiting for Ford to do something irritating, but it never came, not even another kick against my chair. He knew what he was doing, that stupid game he had going on, and I had let him see how it affected me. Well, I knew it wasn't going to happen again.

I waved goodbye to Keeley and Sarah after exchanging numbers in each other's phones so that we could get together for a study group. I took my time packing up my laptop, knowing that my next class was in an hour. Behind me, I could hear the kitten-like purrs from some of the students lingering around Ford, each of them wanting his attention. I could almost ignore it – almost - until one of the eager vixens slid in front of Ford's seat, knocking the back of my head with her leather bag.

I stood with a huff, rolling my eyes so far in the back of my head that I could almost hear my mother shouting from Alaska that my eyes would stay that way. Carefully I strolled to the door, not wanting to trip over my own feet and give them something else to gawk and stare at — no reason to add more ammunition to their arsenal. I didn't dare look back as I exited even though I could feel his stare on me with each step. It made me feel.

. .uncomfortable. As if he could see a part of me that I didn't want anyone to witness. Each passing second peeled away more layers that I'd kept tightly wrapped beneath my skin.

Finally, I was free and I briskly walked toward the stairwell that would take me to the small coffee shop on the first floor. I needed caffeine and I needed it now.

The line was long, but that was fine with me. All I wanted was to slip in the masses and disappear.

Knowing that I had some time to kill, I pulled out my phone and flipped through some social media pages. Nothing overly exciting, though I did get lost in a few animal videos, barely noticing when the line ahead of me moved.

"You ran out of class pretty fast."

I screamed as his breath feathered across my cheek, dropping my phone in the process.

"Oh, fudgesicles," I murmured as I bent down to grab my phone, thankful to find that the screen hadn't cracked.

"Fudgesicles?" Ford mimicked as I stood up and took a step to follow the moving line. He did the same with me.

Taking a deep breath, I worked to recenter myself as I turned to face him. Taking in his blue eyes and the light scruff on his chiseled chin, I couldn't help but notice how attractive he was - again.

"What, are you stalking me now?" I bit out, my attitude toward him seething from my words.

"Don't flatter yourself, princess."

Princess? I was no darn princess.

"Don't call me that," I fumed, narrowing my eyes at him as I took another step in line. I was next and I couldn't wait to get out of here. "And you're the one standing next to me in line. Don't want any of your lady friends to get the wrong idea."

"Maybe I was already behind you in line."

Darn, maybe he was right. I had been so busy on my phone, I hadn't noticed who had joined the line behind me.

"But," he began as he leaned closer to my ear, "I really wanted to see if you always kept that stick up your ass or just wore it to class."

My jaw unclenched as he pulled away. I had never been spoken to that way. Had no idea how to react. So when the barista asked me for my order, I stood there slack-jawed. Only Ford's chuckle brought me back to the moment.

In a daze, I told the barista, "I'll have a medium chai tea latte, please."

Piping in, his body never turning away from mine, Ford added, "I'll have a small black coffee."

At his arrogance, I rolled my eyes while reaching into my wallet for the cash I had on hand, only to find Ford handing the barista a card.

"I've got them."

"Don't be a gentleman on my account."

As the barista handed the card back to Ford and we took two steps to the right to wait for our order, Ford said, "You said so yourself that I was no gentleman."

I should have taken a moment to apologize and thank him for my coffee, but I couldn't find it in me. He wasn't even particularly nice while I stood there silently.

"If you grind your teeth any more, you're not going to have anything left to chew with."

"What is your deal?" I pointed out, my arms automatically crossed against my chest like a shield for more of his heinous words.

"I was simply pointing out better dental habits."

"No, you're just egging me on."

"Maybe," he responded as he shrugged his shoulders and leaned his tall, muscled frame against the glass case containing a few baked goods. "Actually, I do have one more question."

The rolling of my eyes was completely involuntary. "What's that?"

"What do you wear underneath that dress, princess? Are you all prim and proper like you want everyone to believe, or is there a little sex kitten tucked away wearing leather and lace?"

I was affronted. Never in my life had I been spoken to in such a manner and I had been through hell before, but it was never disguised as a gorgeous man in black jeans and a white shirt pulled taut across his chest.

Thankfully the barista placed our orders on the counter at that moment.

Before he could react, I reached for both cups while saying, "Don't worry. You'll never get the pleasure of knowing what I wear beneath my clothes or if I wear anything at all."

I turned to him, smirking and cheering at myself inside as he stood with his lips parted and eyes heated from my words. I knew it would get a reaction out of him, too bad for him it was the truth.

He had barely snapped out of his stupor when he noticed I had moved toward the trash can with his drink in hand.

"Jolee. . ." he warned as my hand hovered over the canister.

"Oops." The paper cup and liquid slipped from my grip and landed with barely a whisper in the trash bag.

"Have a good day, Ford," I told him as I turned around to exit the open area café.

"Bitch," he growled, and the people surrounding us gasped. I wasn't sure if they were surprised at his outburst, the word used, or that someone had spoken to me. Either way, I gave the only response I could. Flicking my middle finger up in the air, I held it to my side proudly while I took a sip of my drink and continued toward my next class.

CHAPTER FOUR

FORD

I stood frozen in place as I stared at Jolee's retreating back, her middle finger flying high in the air. A laugh bubbled out of my chest and then a few more followed suit.

When was the last time that I had laughed?

I couldn't remember. Probably at something one of my brothers did.

That girl knew how to get on my every last nerve without even trying, which was a remarkable feat.

The crowd in the café wasn't sure how to react. I wasn't one to show any emotion. Hell, most of these people had probably never heard a word uttered from me before. Yet, they all knew me. Or, thought that they did. My brothers and I knew that the student body placed us on a pedestal. Not because our mother was a professor here, but because of how we looked. But, hey, I wasn't complaining. Especially when the barista silently handed me another black coffee and an apology.

A few girls eyed me, hoping that I'd shoot them a wink or one of my famous smirks, but they'd get neither, I had other things on my mind. And this time, not even the blonde-haired witch was going to distract me.

Heading out of the building, I made my way off campus and toward the small strip of businesses. My next class wasn't until the afternoon, which left me plenty of time to take the next step of my plan.

The small trinket shop on the corner came into view and I slipped inside. Other college students milled about, but there was one person in mind that I was looking for. Brent Daughtry was a private investigator that used to work with Adam. Link had kept in touch with our adoptive father's police friends. Brent had worked on the force with Adam but had recently branched out on his own.

I needed information and he was the only one I trusted to keep his trap shut. Not even my brothers knew what I had been up to.

"Brent," I greeted as I saw the gray-haired man standing by a shot glass display.

In a surprising gesture, he turned around and greeted me with an embrace. He was the same age Adam would have been and I tried hard not to let the hug bring back any memories. My emotions needed to stay on lockdown.

"Hey, kid. Look at you. My goodness, you've grown up. I bet the ladies love you," he said with his strong Bostonian accent. "How you doin'?"

"Hanging in there. It's good to see you, too."

A beat of silence passed between us as he looked me up and down.

"I got some of what you asked for. But, kid, are you sure you want to get tied up in this?"

"I need to know the truth and so do a lot of other people. If you can't stand with me, I understand."

"No, no, I'm with you. One hundred percent. But maybe you should talk to Tracy about this."

"I know what I'm doing," I pointed out, the short nails on my fingers digging into my palms as I clenched my hands into fists, but I felt no pain. I hadn't felt anything but fury for so long that I wouldn't recognize it even if I bled from the wounds.

Brent nodded as he reached behind him, pulling a folded manila envelope from his back pocket.

"There is a lot of twisted shit in there and I barely broke the surface. He has his fingers into every agency in the state, so he knows how to cover his tracks."

"How were you able to find it?" I asked as I took the envelope from him.

"I'm better at my job than they are. Look, read it over. Call me and we can figure out the next path. I agree with you that you need to know the truth, but just consider how those truths will affect others."

I ignored his comment as I pinned him with my gaze.

"So, what can you tell me so far?"

"There is rumbling in the media that your father's senate seat may not be so steady for the next election. If this information became public, he'd be ruined."

These were things I already knew. It was why I had called him to begin investigating.

"What about my mother?"

"I'm still waiting on a contact to get back with me, but I have a lead and it's looking promising."

The store clerk looked over at us at that moment and I knew that we were drawing unwanted attention. We needed to wrap this up and fast.

"Thanks for this," I told him, smacking the manila envelope against my hand. "Call me anytime."

Brent nodded once, the corners of his eyes tilted downward. I could tell that he was disappointed at the fact I wanted to continue moving forward. But I needed answers.

And most of all, my mother needed justice.

Rutherford Hastings was going down and he wasn't going to know what hit him until it was too late.

I spent my last two classes in a daze. The envelope stuffed firmly in my bag beckoned me to open it and it took every ounce of willpower to keep from reaching for the papers while the professor droned on about class expectations.

Beneath my palm, I twisted the knob to the apartment I shared with Link and Archer; Chance and Rylan shared their own. The aromatic smell of marinara, oregano, and basil filled the air and I closed my eyes to inhale the sweet scent. Archer must be cooking tonight. He always favored the Italian dishes.

"Spaghetti will be ready in ten. You get dish duty tonight."

"Sounds good," I mumbled as I toed my shoes off at the door (one of Link's rules) and made my way to my bedroom.

The door slammed on its own, as if it understood my urgency to rip through the envelope. But as I pulled it from my bag and placed it on the bed, a heaviness settled on me.

Was this what I should be doing? Did I really want to dig up dirt on my birth father? Get my revenge?

Of course, I fucking did. That man had destroyed too many lives in the name of selfishness. He was a repulsive human being and the world needed to know. It made me thankful that I took after my mother's side of the family, but every time I glanced in the mirror, I was reminded of who helped give me life. Those same steely blue eyes stared back at me as a picture of my father on the cover of TIME Magazine rested on my desk. Just looking at the picture surged a wave of hatred through me.

Slumping down on the edge of my bed, I flipped the envelope open and, with shaking hands, pulled out the contents. Beneath a metal paperclip were pictures, letters, transcripts, and news articles related to my father.

Woman upon woman graced the images with my birth father. None of which were my mother or his wife of thirty years. Some, they were merely kissing. Others were more explicit.

My eyes skimmed through the letters, many just day to day correspondences until familiar handwriting lined the pages. It was a letter from my mother. I couldn't bring myself to read it, feeling too much like an invasion of her privacy. But the way her perfect cursive flowed like the petals of a flower, I knew that it was a love letter. A love letter to the man that would break her heart with his lies and false promises.

"Dinner's ready!" Archer called out from the other side of my door.

Just as I was about to stuff the papers back into the envelope, a document with official letterhead caught my attention. The date was the day after my mother's letter was sent. Most of the official documents were written in print by who I assumed was his secretary, but this one was written in manly scribble. Barely legible, but one sentence was scrawled in angry, harsh lettering.

Get the situation with the woman taken care of NOW!

My mother was not a "situation," and if I had had any doubts before about proceeding, that all fell to the wayside in that moment.

"Ford!" Archer shouted again and I dropped the paper back on my bed as I piled the rest of the contents in neatly then placed it on the desk.

I hoped that Brent would come through, but I looked forward to the reading material ahead of me.

Just as Archer finished loading up our plates, Link, Chance, and Rylan, came through the door. Though my other brothers rented an apartment next door, we all took turns cooking meals.

It was strange, none of us were blood-related, with the exception of me and Tyler who were cousins, but we were closer than most families I knew. We always had each other's back. Maybe it was because we'd all seen the worst in people, or maybe it was because we were grateful for the love Tracy and Adam had given us, but for whatever reason, we knew that we would always be there for each other, no matter what. Which made keeping my secret harder. I told them everything, just as they did the same. We had no secrets in our brotherhood. The guilt was nipping away, day by day, but I couldn't tell them. Not yet. Not until I had everything in line.

Together we gathered around the oversized dining table capable of seating ten, but only having chairs for eight. We were large men that liked our space and made sure to keep a chair for Tracy and Tyler whenever they stopped by. Chance and Rylan had a matching set at their apartment. It took up a lot of space in the living room, but somehow Tracy made it work when she helped us set it all up last year.

A television played the news in the background and I could see a clip related to politics rolling across the screen. My hand subconsciously tightened around the neck of the fork I was holding.

"Alright, kids, how was everyone's first day of school?" Link asked as he reached for a piece of garlic bread, breaking my stare from the television. Link was the oldest, and since Adam's passing, he took it upon himself to carry the father-type role, even though he was only a few years older than any of us.

Instead of answering, Archer chucked a balled-up napkin in his direction. Link swatted it away as he took a hefty bite from his bread.

"Heard someone had a run-in with a pretty blonde at the econ building café this morning," Chance said as he slurped his noodles into his mouth.

"Heard that, too," Archer replied as he pointed at me with the prongs of his fork. "Also heard that you bought her drink."

I knew people in the café would talk, but I didn't expect the third degree from my brothers.

"What are you implying?" I asked as I scooped some pasta sauce onto my noodles and took a piece of bread, wishing this conversation would end.

"I'm just telling you what I heard. We've never known you to be interested in a girl. Bed them? Sure. But buy them a drink? No way," Rylan piped in.

"I'm not interested and I didn't buy her a drink just because. I knew it would piss her off to buy it, that's all. And if you must know she dumped my drink in the trash can before she ceremoniously flipped me off as she left."

Nothing but silence met my ears. My brothers stared at me with a mix of confusion, awe, and surprise as I took another large bite of spaghetti.

As if a light bulb went off in Link's head, he smiled. And it wasn't just any smile. It was one of those wicked smiles that grew by the second and usually ended with one of us getting into heaps of trouble.

"You like her."

My head had never spun so quickly as I turned toward him. "I can't fucking stand her. First, she bitched at me in the stairwell when I didn't pick up her luggage that *she* had dropped and knocked into me with. Then she took my seat in class. MY FUCKING SEAT!" I shouted. "She has a stick lodged so far in her ass that I don't even think doctors could remove it." My chest moved up and down as I seethed in my seat. Long gone was my appetite at remembering the witch living above us.

"Yep, he likes her," Archer said, then the other brothers chimed in with their agreements.

Standing from my seat at the table, I grabbed my plate and made my way toward the trash can. "Fuck you all," I said as I left them at the table and locked myself in my bedroom.

I had far better things to do than think about Jolee Ward and the evil she was concocting above me.

RENEE HARLESS

CHAPTER FIVE

JOLEE

Sunshine beamed through the window, bathing my room in a soft glow. I had stayed late into the night at the animal shelter with one of their new arrivals. The abused puppy was skittish of any human that came near him - any human except me. We instantly bonded and I was the only one that could calm him down. If we were allowed to have pets, I definitely would have brought him home.

But even though I was functioning on just a few hours of sleep, I had been looking forward to this day for the last month. It was the Friday before our college fall break. Both Haley and Willow were heading up north to go skiing for the five days. They had invited me, but I'd declined. Not because of my lacking funds, but because

I'd miss seeing the animals at the shelter. And I was secretly looking forward to some quiet time in the apartment.

Looking over at my stack of books, I smiled, knowing that I had one last day doing my best to ignore Ford and his lackeys. I'd made sure to get to the economics class before him and it never failed that he walked in right before the professor would lock the door. Ford would stand at the end of my row and claim that I was in his seat, then move into the seat directly behind me, kicking the back of my chair in the process. He reminded me of the naughty boy in kindergarten that would tug on the pretty girl's pigtails or braids during recess because he secretly liked her. The only difference was that Ford and I couldn't stand each other. If we were called on in class, we made it a point to counter-argue against the other. It was juvenile, but neither of us could resist it. Even Ford's harem and wannabes had started joining in.

Thank goodness for Sarah and Keeley. They were the only ones that ever took my side and seemed to be the only other students on campus that would hang out with me, besides Willow and Haley. In my other classes, everyone stayed at least one desk distance from me. At first, I had felt humiliated, but then I stopped caring.

There was no reason why any of these students should dislike me, especially if they only based their dislike on Ford's reaction toward me. So when I'd arrive at classes, I made it a point to put my belongings in those empty chairs. It was my way of showing them that it didn't bother me anymore.

I no longer stood out in my clothes, using my most recent paycheck to do some damage at Target. It may not have been the luxury items my classmates wore, but they were stylish nonetheless, and I felt more like myself when I wore them.

Glancing at my phone, I noted that I had an hour before I needed to be on campus. Forcing myself out of bed, I rushed through a quick shower and threw on a pair of skinny jeans with a soft gray T-shirt. Twisting my damp hair into a knot at the back of my head, I made my way down the hall toward the kitchen, where I was surprised to find Willow and Haley both standing at the counter with a cup of coffee. Usually, they were barely out of their beds when it was time for class.

"Good morning," I greeted them as I reached up to grab a mug from the cabinet. I needed my morning sustenance before I could really delve into a conversation. "I'm surprised to see you both up."

"We told you that most students don't show up to classes on the Friday before a break. Heck, I think all but one of my classes was cancelled," Willow said.

Haley took one large gulp of her coffee then rinsed out the cup in the sink before placing it in our dishwasher. Willow did the same, not a minute later.

"We're going to go ahead and head to the resort. Are you sure you don't want to join us?" my cousin asked again, the same as she had the last two weeks. My answer never faltered.

"No, I still have to work this afternoon and I have a study group tonight with Sarah and Keeley."

"I know, I know. Can't say that I didn't try."

Haley piped in, "Be careful by yourself. And no hanky panky in my bedroom." We all giggled together and I felt lighter than I had in years. Moving in with Willow was one of the best things I'd done.

"There would have to be a male interested in me for me to even consider any hanky panky," I added.

"Oh, there are interested boys. But we all know you have your eyes on Ford O'Brien."

"Haley!" I screeched. "I do not have eyes for Ford. He is the most arrogant and self-centered jerk not only on this campus but the entire planet."

"One doth protest too much."

"Willow! Not you, too!"

She simply shrugged her shoulders with a devilish smile and I couldn't help but reach for one of the dishrags on the counter and toss it in the direction of her face.

"Hey!" she cried out.

"Y'all are supposed to be on my side."

"We are!" they barked in unison. Willow added, "If it makes you feel better, there isn't a girl on this campus that hasn't imagined hooking up with Ford or any of the ridge rogues for that matter. You're not alone."

"Except I don't imagine hooking up with Ford," I lied. Of course, I had dreamt of kissing him, everywhere, and him returning the favor. It's actually what I had fantasized about last night. But I didn't want them to know that or I'd never hear the end of it.

"Look how her cheeks are turning red," Willow said as she nudged Haley's arm. "You're imagining hooking up with him right now, aren't you, Jolee?"

I could feel my cheeks flame even hotter as Willow called me out. It was precisely what I was doing in my mind and it was going to make seeing Ford today in class even more unbearable.

"Leave her alone, Willow. We need to get on the road if we want to be at the Canadian border by lunchtime."

"Fine," Willow replied, her voice sounding defeated. She walked over to me and squeezed her arms around me tightly, Haley repeating the motion after Willow took a step back.

"Be safe," I told them as they reached for their suitcases.

"You too!" they called out behind them as the door shut at their exit.

Standing in the middle of my kitchen with a warm cup of coffee in my hand, I glanced around the space. I was tempted to skip my classes and veg out on the couch all day until I had to head to work, but a smile slowly grew on my face as I took a sip of my drink. I couldn't give Ford the satisfaction of being able to sit in my seat. That wouldn't do at all.

Just as the girls had warned, there were only a handful of students in the classroom by the time the professor locked the door. Keeley and Sarah had made it, but I had to work hard to mask my disappointment at Ford's lack of arrival.

I had actually been looking forward to seeing him. The daily seat questioning had become routine and now my day felt out of sorts. It was strange not to feel the constant kicking against the back of my seat, a motion I had grown accustomed to. And when the professor asked me a question about the lecture from the day before, the entire class went silent when there was no one to protest against my answer.

I should have known then that my day was going to be hell. By lunch, I had already considered calling out of work and retreating to Canada with my roommates. I had spilled my daily chai tea latte on my bag and a leg of my jeans. I was thankful the hot liquid didn't burn my leg or ruin my laptop, but I had no time to change before my next class. Good thing no one sat close enough to me to be able to smell the spilled drink on my clothes.

I stopped by the apartment to drop off my bag and damp school supplies before heading into work. Fridays were our short days at the veterinary office, closing at 5 p.m., but I would be there until seven cleaning the cages and completing the weekly inventory. It made me feel good to be helpful since I could only work a few days a week for them.

Dr. Allen greeted me when I arrived through the back entrance. She was still wearing the surgical coverings so I assumed that she had an emergency come in. That was the downfall of being so close to a college town, many of the residents and students didn't or couldn't take care of their animals. The animal shelter was another block down the road and they constantly had students dropping off pets that they couldn't care for, or police bringing in pets that had been left behind.

I quickly went to work cleaning the exam rooms and then the operating room, which took a bit longer than normal, and by the time that I was done, most of their appointments were complete.

Grabbing the food containers, I filled them with the proper amounts for the animals we had on-site. Some were here for surgeries, others for quarantines, and a few were being boarded during the break.

The cats couldn't have cared less when I placed their appropriate food in their crates, but the dogs started barking and jumping in excitement. Their thrill at having a visitor always gave me the same kind of joy.

One of the dogs continued to lay in the corner, barely lifting his head when I opened his door to place his food inside. He was a large German shepherd that was recovering from hip surgery.

"Hey, big guy," I said as I knelt down close to him, making sure to let him sniff my hand before I ran my fingers through his thick coat.

"I know you're not feeling too good, but you should try to eat some food. Don't tell the others, but I mixed some of the yummy wet food in with it."

His right ear perked up just a bit and I had no chance at fighting against my smile.

"Come on, if you eat just a little, I'll see if Dr. Allen can give you some more feel-good juice."

Nudging the bowl closer to his muzzle, I watched as Hercules lifted himself just a little bit so that he could take a few bites of food. He looked at me with what I imagined were his brows raised gesturing for me to get the feel-good juice that Dr. Allen would insert in his IV.

"Good job, buddy." Patting his head once more, I let myself out of the cage in search of Dr. Allen.

I found her sitting at her desk, making some notes in the electronic charts.

"I was able to get Hercules to eat some food. Do you think you could give him some more pain medicine? He seems to be hurting a bit."

She looked surprised at my request and I worried that I had overstepped my boundaries. It wasn't my job to know what kind of care the animal needed.

"You were able to get him to eat?" she said in astonishment. "We've been trying since yesterday morning."

"Yes, he ate about half of the bowl. He likes a little bit of wet food mixed in."

"Wow, yes, of course, I'll get him some pain meds right away. I didn't want to do it on an empty stomach."

"Thank you," I told her and turned to exit the office.

"Jolee?" she called out and my nerves skyrocketed.

Had I done something wrong? Was I in trouble?

"Yes, ma'am?"

Dr. Allen stood from her desk and walked around until she was about a foot away from me.

"You've done a really great job since you started working here and we all have noticed. You're going to run a great animal rescue and sanctuary, let me know if you ever need anything when it gets off the ground, okay?"

I was speechless. When I made calls to see if they were hiring, I had mentioned that my goal was to open a place similar to where I had been working before, but I never imagined that she would remember.

"Wow, thank you. That means. . .that means everything."

"Now, go and enjoy your weekend."

"Thank you, Dr. Allen," I replied as she retreated back behind her desk.

My walk back home felt lighter, as if I was walking on a cloud. Each step felt weightless. By the time I arrived back at my apartment, I only had fifteen minutes until I needed to meet Keeley and Sarah for our study group.

At lightning speed, I changed out of my T-shirt and jeans, opting for a similar outfit that was clean and didn't reek of animal fur and spoiled milk from the spilled latte. I untwisted my hair from its knot and let it fall in soft waves around my shoulders. I didn't need to touch up any makeup because on days when I worked, I went without any. The work in the kennels would have had it melting off my face in record time.

Glancing in my full-length mirror, I took in my appearance. I looked the same, except for my sparkling eyes, which were thanks to Dr. Allen's compliment, but I felt different. Like I was finally figuring out who I was and who I could be. Not just the girl from Alaska with crazy parents.

I slipped my feet into a pair of flats and placed my bag and purse over my shoulder. Just as I was about to leave the apartment, I realized that I had left my phone in the back pocket of my dirty jeans. But when I went to retrieve it, the plastic and metal lit up and then immediately went black, mocking me in my haste. The battery was dead.

I was running late, so I left my phone on my bed, promising myself that I would charge it when I returned from the library, and I skirted out the door as if my feet were on fire. This time I didn't even glance at the third floor in my haste to meet Keeley and Sarah.

The library was empty when I arrived except for my two friends sitting at a small corner table, three paper cups placed in front of them.

"Hey," I called out with a wave, immediately receiving a shushing noise from another student that I hadn't noticed.

I mouthed, "Sorry," to him in apology.

"We got you a coffee," Keeley said as she handed me the extra cup. The warmth of the drink seeped through the paper cup onto my palm and I smiled.

"Thank you. You're both heading home tonight, right?" The dorms closed during the break, and no one was allowed to stay on campus, which meant that Keeley and Sarah were scheduled to head home.

"Yep. We're all packed and ready to go. Don't tell anyone, but I'm actually missing home a bit," Sarah chimed in with her palm raised against her mouth as she divulged her secret.

Making a motion across my chest, I told her, "Your secret is safe with me. Did either of you print the study guide for the exam?"

Keeley nodded and handed out three copies and we spent the next two hours reviewing the material until our eyes crossed.

Darkness had fallen over the campus, and though shadows were looming around the lamplights that lined the walkways, I found it quite beautiful. I hadn't ventured onto campus at night, spending those late hours volunteering my time, but as I stepped down from the library stairs, I told myself that I should try to stroll around campus more often.

I waved at the campus officer that walked passed me and he nodded. Other than him, there wasn't anyone milling about that I could see. I started reciting the anagram that Keeley and I came up with to remember some of the points from the study guide. That was why I didn't hear the group of boys sneaking up behind me.

A clammy hand covered my mouth before I could scream or shout just as another hand gripped my arm and tugged me backward into the shadows of a looming building. I reached out for the blue emergency alarm across the pathway, but they were too strong. A boy stood in front of me and reached for my bags, but because they were across my body, he only gathered a chunk of my shirt.

Only a few seconds had passed before I bit down on the hand covering my mouth. The boy cursed loudly against my ear. I swung my arms and kicked my legs wildly to keep them from reaching for me again, but lost my balance and fell to the ground. My backside ached at the fall on the cold, rough ground and I found myself fighting against the blackness, remembering how I had felt this before.

One of the men tried again to reach for my bags while the man with the clammy hands yanked at my arm and kicked my stomach. I didn't have time to react after my fall and they were counting on my lack of fight to steal my belongings. I started screaming   for help, but no one seemed to come to my rescue.

Another shadow figure closed in and hovered over the man grabbing for my purse in the darkness. With a quick punch, the smaller figure fell away. I watched in awe as the larger man did the same to the other two men and they quickly joined their friend in a heap on the ground. Collectively they scurried backward like crabs until they could regain their balance and run off down the deserted pathway. I squinted my eyes as they passed by a lamppost, but I couldn't make them out.

"Are you okay?" the deep voice asked and I jolted in response.

It was the man from the stairwell, the one with his hair tied back. I remembered Willow saying his name was Link.

He didn't wait for my response. Instead, he squatted in front of me and leaned in close. "You're in shock," he whispered. "Did they hurt you?"

"No, I. . .I don't think so."

Even in the dimness, I could see the relief wash over his face at my response. Link stood again and reached a hand out to help me up. I was grateful for the assistance because I could barely collect enough energy to stand.

He reached down to the ground and gathered my school bag, which contained my laptop and notes. I prayed that I would be able to salvage both. My cloth purse, on the other hand, was ripped in two, the contents spilled on the ground. Link did his best to collect what he could see and shoved the items into my school bag.

"Thank you," I murmured, hating how afraid I felt and sounded. He walked over to the emergency call button and spoke with the operator. Soon the officer that had passed me earlier joined us. He was disappointed that I couldn't give him a description of my assailants, but he took down my information, promising to get back with me if he had any leads. He suspected that they weren't students while I was grateful that nothing worse had happened.

I know that after what had just happened, I should be fearful of standing alone with Link on a dark pathway, but something told me that he wouldn't hurt me.

"Let me walk you home. I was heading back to the apartment myself."

"Thanks. I appreciate it." I tried to smile, but it didn't feel right against my skin. That's when I noticed I was bleeding — the metallic taste lingered on my tongue.

In my alarm, I reached up to my face, touching it gently as I searched for the cut.

"You have a cut on your lip and cheek. They're small, though."

"Oh."

We both stepped away from the building and onto the pathway that would take us back to the apartment building. When we crossed one of the glows from the lamp, I looked up at Link and was surprised that he didn't seem fazed at all from the altercation. Even though his hands still fisted tightly, his clothes didn't have a single wrinkle, and his hair was neatly styled back in its leather tie.

"Were you coming from the library?" he asked as we left campus and began the stroll down dark side toward the apartment.

"Yeah, I had an economics study group."

He answered with a grunt and remained silent the rest of the stroll. Even as we made our way up the stairwell Link stayed quiet, but lingered close to my side.

I expected him to continue toward his apartment when we reached the third floor, but he resumed the journey up the next flight with me.

"You don't have to walk me. I'll be okay," I insisted as we turned onto the landing.

"I want to make sure you're safe inside your apartment."

With a chuckle, I told him, "Maybe you could give Ford some pointers on how to be a gentleman."

"I'll see what I can do."

We approached my apartment door and I dug through my school bag in search of my keys only to come up empty-handed.

No. No. No.

Hastily I dumped the contents of the bag on the ground only to groan when the jingle of keys was nowhere to be heard.

Tears blossomed along my bottoms lids as I looked up at Link.

"Are either of your roommates home?" he asked gently, most likely trying to keep me from having a breakdown. No one wanted to witness that.

"No, they went skiing for fall break, and to make matters worse, my phone was dead when I left, so it's in my room." My heart started pounding in my chest and I knew that I was on the verge of a freakout. I felt helpless and defeated.

Chaotically I started throwing the items strewn on the dingy floor into my bag only to have Link place a hand over mine. He was wordlessly asking me to calm down. I took a deep breath and slowly put the rest of the items back into my bag and stood.

"Come with me. You can stay at our place for the night and I'll call the leasing agency to get a new lock installed for you tomorrow."

"You don't have to do that," I spoke softly, gripping the strap of my bag as it rested against my chest.

"That's what friends do. Come on, it's almost dinnertime."

Following him down the steps, I inquired, "Dinner? It's almost 10 p.m."

"We like to eat dinner together and they were waiting for me."

Stopping at the small landing between the flight of stairs where the direction shifted, he held out his hand to me. "I'm Link, by the way. I don't think we've been formally introduced."

It was strange to meet someone that you knew more about simply based on their reputation. Shifting my hand into his, I replied, "Jolee. And, thank you, for today."

Warmth radiated from his growing smile, a deep contrast against the harsh lines of his brows. Though Link had an air of anger and fury surrounding him, he left me feeling nothing but kindness. As if that was his defense mechanism to keep people at arm's length.

Finally, we arrived at the door to his apartment – 306.

"Hey, guys," he called out as he opened the door, waving his hand to beckon me inside. "Stay here," he murmured. "I want to make sure that, well, that they aren't being shitheads." I didn't know what he meant since I had never been into a boy's apartment before, but I could only imagine it could mean certain states of nakedness and women. My uncertainty about the situation continued to grow as I was left waiting. But I had nowhere else to go. No friends to call on except for a few people that I worked with, but that would require my phone since there was zero chance I could remember their phone numbers.

Link reappeared seconds later and my nerves were shot. I was about to be thrust into the den of hungry lions without a way to protect myself. Somehow I always found myself in these types of situations. My teeth were digging into my lip as he stepped forward, the newly acquired cut aching, but I couldn't stop.

"Hey, it's okay. I told them that I had a friend that needed a place to crash for the night."

He gently placed a hand on the middle of my back, guiding me farther into the apartment.

"Did you tell them who I was?" I said through a tight whisper. I had the urge to dig my heels into the floor and halt my descent into hell.

"No, I didn't think. . ." Link began until a roar from the kitchen pulled his attention.

"What the fuck is she doing here?"

CHAPTER SIX

FORD

Tonight was my night for dinner, and since it was Friday, I opted for pizza – the homemade kind. I had just pulled the third pizza out of the oven when Link walked into the kitchen. At first glance, nothing about him seemed more harried than usual, but his eyes filled with worry and concern.

Shit, did he find out about Brent and my father?

I could only imagine the kind of talking to Link would give me over that – the kind of talking where his fist communicated with my face. I could hold my own in a fight, spending most of my free time at the gym down the street, but Link was a prized fighter. I didn't want to be around when he lost it.

"Hey," he spoke in a low voice. "I have a friend with me that needs a place for the night."

I eyed him skeptically. Leave it to Link and his hero complex to help someone in need.

"They're not going to rob the place, are they?"

Link smiled and I began to worry about who he actually brought home. We'd never seen him bring back a woman, opting to go to her place instead. But there was a first for everything.

"No, I think we're safe."

Turning my back to him, I moved toward the fridge to grab us all a drink. A bottle of water for Link, Chance, and Rylan. A beer for Archer and me. As I finished popping the cap off of my bottle of Bud Light, Link strolled into the living room with a woman. And not just any woman. It was my nemesis - Jolee.

"What the fuck is she doing here?" I shouted as the bottle began to slip from my hands. Quickly I placed it on the counter and stomped toward them.

Her hair was draped over her face, the long blonde waves mocked me as they skimmed her breasts covered by the gray T-shirt.

"Link? What the fuck, man?" My voice howled in the room and Jolee flinched with every word.

"She's locked out of her apartment."

"And she has roommates," I retorted, pretending as hard as I could that Jolee wasn't standing within arm's reach.

"Everyone's left for break, man."

Unleashing a fountain of fury, Jolee turned her face toward me, her long hair smacking my arm in the process. A hint of black smudges lined the skin beneath her lower lashes, but I couldn't pull my gaze away from the ferocity in her eyes directed toward me.

"I'm standing right here, you know. Why don't you just ask me what I'm doing in your apartment?"

I smiled. I couldn't help it. Jolee had appeared so weak and fragile when she had arrived, and here she was, a ticking time bomb ready to explode. Her body grew even more rigid at my grin and I was very tempted to see if I could get her control to snap.

That was when I noticed the blood on her lip. It looked to be from a recent cut and some scratches along her face. One of the scratches was deep enough that it would need the liquid stitches Link kept in the first aid kit. On impulse, I reached out and cupped her jaw in my palm, twisting her head side to side taking in her injuries. I dragged my eyes up and down her body, noting the small tears in her shirt and dirt smattered along her jeans.

Our eyes locked, hers filled with rage and mine filled with confusion, and a beat of silence passed between us. My hand fell from her face as she jerked her head to the side, breaking our connection, and I let that rejection fuel my anger at her being our problem now.

"What happened?"

Narrowing her eyes in my direction, Jolee's grip around the strap across her chest tightened. "I was assaulted leaving the library. They either ran off with my keys or they're lying in the bushes. I don't have my phone because it was dead and I left it in my apartment. Everyone I know on campus has gone home and I have nowhere else to go." Her voice grew louder with every word until she was shouting and I was mesmerized by the small flare of her nostrils. She was beautiful to begin with, but when she was angry, man, she was fucking gorgeous.

"Pizza! Yes!" Archer exclaimed as he walked out of his bedroom into the kitchen, breaking the tension in the room.

Link, Jolee, and I stood in the living space with our stares locked on each other. Mine on Jolee's, which she vehemently returned, and Link's on me, probably trying to figure out what I had against his female guest.

"She's staying, Ford," Link stated, not leaving any room for argument, just as Archer noticed our new arrival.

"Well," Archer said, prolonging each consonant. "I'm guessing by the way that Ford has turned an interesting shade of red, that you must be the woman that pissed him off on the first day of school."

Jolee's shoulders deflated as if she expected Archer to throw her out simply because she had been cast on the wrong side by his brother, but I knew what he was up to. "Probably," she replied.

"Oh man, this is great. Tell me all about how you made an enemy of our dear brooding brother. Come sit beside me." Archer gestured to the chair that I usually sat in, which was beside his.

Great. Just fucking great. She was going to stay and there wasn't shit I could do about it. No one could turn down the Archer charm.

I watched as Jolee slipped an invisible mask over her emotions; that anger she so easily spewed in my direction now locked tight away. She smiled at Archer and turned to do the same to Link before knocking against me with her shoulder as she walked toward the table.

"Come sit down. It's just for a night." Link patted my shoulder as he walked into the kitchen to grab his water and plated two slices of pizza for himself.

Archer and Link were digging into their food, and because I was a fucking saint, I plated two slices of pizza for Jolee, two for myself, and balanced them and the two beers in my hands as I carried them to the table.

I smirked triumphantly when Jolee looked across the table at me in surprise. "Did you poison it?"

"Not this time. Just eat," I growled before sitting and taking an extra-large bite of the doughy goodness.

From behind my lashes, I watched her lift the slice hesitantly and bring it to her mouth. I was surprised when she took a regular-sized bite expecting her to take the tiniest if only to check that I indeed wasn't trying to kill her. Her eyes widened in surprise as she looked down at the masterpiece I created.

"Oh my goodness, this is amazing," she exclaimed before taking another bite. With her hand covering her mouth, she asked, "What brand is it?"

Both Link and Archer chuckled at her question before taking another bite of their dinner.

"I made it from scratch, princess."

In amazement, Jolee looked back and forth between me and the slice in her hand, the soft skin between her brows crinkling. I wanted to reach out and smooth the wrinkles.

"It's fantastic. How is that even possible?"

"I'm more than just a pretty face," I told her sarcastically, loving how her cheeks reddened.

From beside her, Archer knocked her arm with his elbow to get her attention.

"So, tell me what it was like to flip off Ford O'Brien and live to tell the tale?"

My triumph was short-lived as Chance and Rylan chose that moment to join us and our new companion went on to tell my brothers about all the instances she got the upper hand on me. I should have been embarrassed, but I couldn't peel my eyes away from her animated storytelling. She had us all fascinated.

The phone stuffed in my pants pocket began vibrating against my leg and I immediately left the table without a word. Brent was calling to go over some of the newest information he had emailed over. More letters and documentation of his affairs, but nothing concrete regarding my mother or my cousin's parents.

Ending the phone call, I held my head in my hands, my elbows rested on the rough wooden surface of my desk. The call had me questioning my path, if it was going to get me the revenge I so needed. Wiping my hands against my face, I felt defeated at the prospect of failing. Noting the time, I slammed the laptop closed and made my way out into the living room.

While I had locked myself away in my bedroom for two hours, my brothers had done the same. Jolee was sitting on the couch, her knees against her chest as she stared at the television. When she noticed that I had walked into the room, she immediately diverted her eyes. She looked about as uncomfortable as I felt with the situation.

"Need a blanket or pillow?" I asked as I flicked off the light in the kitchen.

"No, I'm fine. I'll probably stay up anyway."

She couldn't see me roll my eyes at her defiance. My brothers thought I was stubborn, but I had met my match with this girl.

"Okay, suit yourself."

Casually I strolled to the bathroom, glancing over my shoulder before I closed the door to steal another glimpse of the blue and white light illuminating Jolee's face. I hated how attractive I found her. It messed with my head and I didn't need the distraction.

I brushed my teeth and washed my face to get ready for bed then made my way back to my bedroom, forcing myself not to glance back into the living room.

I chucked off my pants and shirt, leaving myself clad in black boxer briefs before slipping between the navy colored cotton sheets of my bed. My mind wouldn't slow down and kept sifting through the new information about my sperm donor. I tossed and turned until finally lying on my back, staring up at the ceiling. Then an image of Jolee flickered in my mind. Her cut lip, her scratched face, the bruises that were forming against her cheek, the torn clothes. What had she been through? My body launched from the bed. I was angry. Angry that something had happened to her. Angry that she was here invading my space and I didn't get a say. Angry that I cared.

I stomped out of my bedroom and toward the living room. At some point, she had turned the television off and basked the room in darkness. It took a moment for my eyes to adjust, but I found her lying on her side, curled into a ball.

My body was possessed as I bent in front of her and lifted her into my arms.

"What are you doing?" she asked and I heard the slightest catch in her voice from a sob. Fuck, she had been crying. My hands instinctively tightened their hold on her.

Between clenched teeth, I replied, "You're not sleeping on the fucking couch. If you're going to sleep, you'll sleep in an actual bed." Unceremoniously I dropped her on the opposite side of my bed, sneering as she bounced.

"I don't want to sleep in your bed. You'll probably try to suffocate me."

I moved to my side of the bed in the blackness and slipped between the sheets again.

"Not today, princess. Then I'd have no one to argue with."

I chuckled at her answering growl and turned my body away so that my back was facing her. The bed moved up and down as she tried to settle into place. Finally, the mattress stopped shifting and I closed my eyes, thankful that my mind seemed clear.

Sleep was claiming me swiftly and I was falling under its spell when I heard the faintest whisper. "Thank you, Ford."

I knew that I should probably respond; that was the gentlemanly thing to do. But as Jolee claimed, I was no gentleman. And she was turning into a disruption that could ruin everything.

On instinct, I woke at 5 a.m. since that was the time that I usually headed to the gym. My body turned toward Jolee, and as if my brain knew that I would be tempted to touch her in my sleep, my arms tightened across my chest. The sheet was pooled at my waist but wrapped tightly around Jolee's body. Mounds of hair covered her face and I reached out, gently sliding the silky strands behind her.

She looked serene in her state of sleep, her full pink lips softly parted as she exhaled. My touch lingered longer than I intended and as I tucked my hand back under my arm she moved slightly. I couldn't look away, wondering how someone could sleep so peacefully. I always had too much on my mind to succumb to a night of full and dreamless sleep, but regardless of what Jolee had been through the night before, she seemed to feel safe enough to sleep in my bed.

Her lips moved slightly as if she was speaking to someone in her dream and I couldn't turn away. I wondered what it would be like to taste those lips, to nibble at the soft skin, to feel my tongue slip between them. And I hated myself for that wayward thinking, it was turning me into someone I didn't know, someone I could never be.

She chose that moment to open her eyes, blinking a few times as she remembered where she was. With her defenses long forgotten, Jolee gazed at me in a way that I recognized, that familiar heady glaze longing for a kiss. Except I couldn't allow myself to let her any closer.

Turning over, I sat up and placed my feet on the floor, giving her a view of my bare back. "Go back to sleep," I bit out as I stood, glancing around my room for my discarded jeans, eyeing them at the foot of the bed. I angrily tugged them on, leaving the top button unclasped.

It wasn't until I reached for my phone that I noticed her hurt expression. I didn't know what to say because I wasn't at liberty to make her feel better. Thankfully she turned back over and faced the window, making sure to tug extra hard on the sheets.

I left the room in a hurry, treading heavily into the bathroom to relieve myself, then made my way to the kitchen. I had a nagging feeling that I had screwed up and karma was making sure that I completely understood the ramifications. When I went to start the coffee maker, the container of grounds spilled at my feet as I popped the lid. Then when I went to grab the broom to clean up, I pinched my finger closing the closet door. While I was busy cursing my lousy luck, Link chose that moment to walk into the kitchen as if he had had the best sleep of his life.

"I got a hold of the maintenance guy and he's installing Jolee's new lock as we speak."

Well, that was freaking fast.

"Where is she, by the way?"

"I let her sleep in my room." I scowled up at him.

"Mmhmm. That's an interesting turn of events."

With a final scoop into the dustpan, I stood and dumped its contents into the trash.

"I know what you're doing, Link."

"Do you?" he asked. He wanted me to question myself, wanted me to change my no dating rule in favor of a particular blonde neighbor.

"Yes, I-," I began until said blonde marched into the living room and looked around the space aimlessly. "You're supposed to be sleeping." I was hot, but not the good kind. The kind that made me want to lift her over my shoulder and toss her back into my bedroom until those dark smudges under her eyes disappeared.

"Well, I'm not. And to be honest, I'd like to make sure that no one sees me or gets the idea that I willingly spent the night here." Reaching down, Jolee bent at the waist before standing up with her bag in hand. "Did you say the maintenance man was installing my lock now?" She looked at Link specifically and he nodded in response, probably as shocked as I was to feel the full wrath of her venom. "Great. Thank you for saving me," Jolee said as she lifted on her toes and pressed her lips against Link's cheek.

Clenching my hands into fists, I realized that I might kill my brother as we watched her open our door and leave the apartment.

We both stood there silently, long after she left. She had taken my cruelty and thrown it back at me.

"What the hell just happened?"

With a heavy sigh, I finally unclenched my fists as I said, "I gave her a reason to hate me again."

My older brother, the one who taught me right from wrong and how to properly throw a punch, turned toward me, his face full of disdain and disappointment.

I kept my secrets close to my chest, but my family knew that I never wanted to get tangled up with a woman. A quick lay? Sure? But a serious relationship? That was not in the cards. I had major trust issues, and the more I learned of my birth father, the more I was afraid that the deck wasn't ever going to deal in my favor.

"She'd like her."

"Tracy likes everyone."

"She does, but I wasn't talking about her. I was talking about your mom," Link added as he sat down on the couch, gripped the remote control, and turned on the television.

But fuck if he wasn't right. Mom would love the fire in Jolee.

And that just gave me another reason to stay away.

RENEE HARLESS

CHAPTER SEVEN

JOLEE

It had been two weeks since I stormed away from Ford's apartment. Nothing had changed; he was still as irritating as ever, doing whatever he could to get a rise out of me. I couldn't wait for Thanksgiving, for no other reason than I wouldn't have to see his gorgeous face for a few days.

Growing up, I had always been friendly, even to the school bully, never giving anyone a reason to be unkind toward me. Of course, that all changed in high school when David moved to our town. He was not only the new guy, but he was all-American beautiful. Blond hair and blue eyes, large build – he was a teen heartthrob. And he was popular from day one. When he showed interest in me, the average girl in his homeroom, everything changed. The girls became catty and vicious, and I learned that if I tried to ignore them, things only got worse. So I quickly learned how to turn the tables.

I shuddered at the thought of how much worse things had transpired. It was why I desperately needed out of our town in Anchorage. My parents didn't understand, but they had other things on their mind. Anything having to do with me was always a second thought.

Joe's Diner was just on the outskirts of campus and it was where Sarah, Keeley, and I met for lunch on the days we had economics together, but they were both sick with the stomach bug going around the school. It seemed that almost everyone had been on the receiving end of the virus — everyone except me, Ford, and a couple of students. Even with the room nearly empty this morning, he still made it a point to sit in the seat directly behind me and irritate me throughout the lecture. He had resorted to not just kicking my chair, but leaning over his small desk and poking my shoulder with his pen.

Keeley had asked me on numerous occasions why I didn't just move over one more chair, but I explained to her that it was the principle of the thing. And at this point in the game, I was pretty sure that he would simply move behind wherever I sat.

Since I left his apartment, I had tried to think of a way to apologize to Link. He had been gracious and caring, after all. I had considered making him dinner or baking him a dessert and dropping it off at his apartment, but the thought of running into Ford outside of class was too much.

To be honest, I wasn't sure how I would react if we were in close confines again. I was fairly certain I would either smack Ford or spew hateful words that I couldn't take back. My embarrassment from that morning wouldn't allow me to consider any other options.

Leaning back in the chair, the wrought iron of the café chair digging into my back, I recalled waking up in his bed. I had woken up about an hour earlier, my body not used to getting so much sleep, and gazed at him. Even in the bleakness of night, I could see how peaceful and serene Ford appeared, the anger that he carried and weighed him down long forgotten. He was a beautiful man, and with his defenses down, I could truly see the kind of man he could be lurking just beneath the surface. I had fallen back to sleep with a small grin on my face and dreamt of him. When I woke again, I was still partly lost in my vision and yearned for the kiss that was about to take place. Except, the Ford staring back at me was real, and yet, I still wanted his kiss. I wasn't surprised that he turned down my silent plea. And when he stormed from the room, I had been furious and surprised at myself. He was mean and callous on most days, so his reaction wasn't unrealistic. But I had no desire to be one of Ford's hanger-ons. I had dreams of my own, big plans that needed my focus, and they didn't involve an attention-seeking boy.

Reaching down I searched through my bag for my notebook and a pen, wanting to add to my notes for the rescue I planned to open one day, but just as I bent forward, someone knocked into my chair causing it to jerk and my head to collide with the edge of the table.

"Son of a beach," I cried out, forgetting the notebook and pen as I pressed my hand to my head.

I spun around quickly in my chair, which brought me face to face with my nemesis sitting in a chair at the table behind me.

"So, what? We're moving on to physical harm now?" I argued, the throbbing of the goose egg forming beneath my scalp immediately caused my head to ache.

Ford shrugged his shoulders innocently. "All I did was nudge your chair accidentally."

"Accidentally?"

"And maybe that guy over there was headed your way." He pointed with his chin toward a man in a red shirt, his back to me. "He isn't your type."

My stare lingered on the man's back. I may not have needed a relationship, but a night of sex didn't sound too bad.

Turning back to Ford, who gazed at me smugly, I said, "So, you're now giving relationship advice? Well, let me clue you in, Ford O'Brien, that I have zero desire for a boyfriend." My voice was escalating as I spoke and I was drawing the attention of the few students surrounding us, but I didn't care. "Maybe what I want is a night of hot sex. Did you ever consider that?" My brain had wanted to say, "With you," but I stopped before I could make that colossal mistake. If Ford even had the slightest inkling of the things that I imagined doing with him, to him, he would use it to his advantage.

"Enjoy your lunch, Ford. I've now lost my appetite."

Somehow I managed to carry my head high as I walked away from the open-air café. But the moment I turned the corner, my shoulders slouched, and my feet dragged. Arguing with Ford was exhausting, probably because it wasn't my usual MO. Hopefully, we'd only have a few more weeks of being in each other's presence.

Of course, knowing Ford, he'd find a way to terrorize me. Probably making sure he's in at least one of my classes every semester.

Irritated at that thought, I made my way over to my last class of the day, anticipating the late night that I had ahead of me. Being at work meant that there was zero chance of running into Ford for at least a handful of hours. And right now, I needed that reprieve.

Dr. Allen could sense that I needed to lose my mind in trivial work when I arrived and she gave me carte blanche to complete any of the ancillary tasks that the office required. I had never felt so fulfilled vacuuming dog and cat hair or mucking kennels.

That night, I was volunteering at the animal shelter, so I only had a few minutes to grab a quick dinner. I walked down the street and into the fast-food dining room, ordered a cheeseburger, and shoveled it down in record time. I probably looked homeless with a faded shirt and stained jeans, and a large duffle bag that was strewn across my body. The days I worked at the animal shelter, I always showered and changed before leaving. I spent a lot of one on one time with the animals and cleaning and didn't like to bring that into the apartment. The staff didn't seem to mind either because I was more than happy to take care of some of the dirtier tasks that they needed. If I was going to open a rescue one day, I needed to understand all aspects of animal care.

Technicians greeted me the moment I walked through the back door of the shelter and hung up my duffle bag in my locker. A task list was posted on the door for the volunteers and I got to work, marking off the items as I went. It was midnight before one of the overnight technicians got a hold of me.

"Hey, Jolee," Ken called out. He was tall with light brown hair, brown eyes, and a kind smile. Not much older than myself, we spent a lot of time chatting while I worked the later hours. He was attractive in the boy-next-door sort of way, but he was also happily engaged to his high school sweetheart.

"Hey, Ken," I replied as I washed my hands at the back sink after cleaning some of the lab equipment.

"We just got a call about a dog that was hit by a car. The owner is bringing him in. I know you're probably on your way out, but do you think you can stay for a while longer. With the stomach bug going around, we could use an extra hand in surgery."

This was one of those catch-22 moments that I both loved and hated. Being asked to assist or even watch a surgery felt like acing an exam. I loved witnessing doctors work their magic to save an animal's life. But the need for an operation at all broke my heart. I had seen some horrific things in the few years I had been a part of animal medicine, and with my career path, I was sure that I would observe more.

"Sure, Ken. I'd be happy to stay."

"Thanks. You're a lifesaver. I may even share my coveted Cosmic Brownie with you." I burst into giggles as I finished drying my hands. Ken's fiancée packed him the most childish snacks on the planet for his midnight shifts. She wrote the sweetest notes on them, though, and I think that was why he secretly enjoyed them. He never let anyone touch his snacks, so to be offered one was serious business.

The veterinarian on duty was waiting out front to greet the dog owners while Ken and I set up the X-ray and surgery rooms. A combination of excitement and fear pulsed through my veins, and when the doctor wheeled the black Labrador with the gray muzzle back into the surgical space, it skyrocketed.

After the X-rays were taken and the doctor determined the best course for surgery, I donned the appropriate surgical gear while Ken got to work sedating the dog. I knew that there wasn't much assistance I could give during the procedure except hand over a few of the tools, so I spent the majority of the time watching the doctor's skillful hands.

"Let's close it up," the veterinarian said as he finished sewing some of the interior muscles. "This one has a long road ahead, and since he's so old, it doesn't look promising."

Together, Ken and I carried the dog called Rocky to the small kennel he would get to recover in while the doctor went to speak with the owners.

"He should be waking up soon," Ken said as he stood up.

"Can I stay with him? Just until he wakes up."

Ken looked at me skeptically before agreeing. I tried my hardest not to grow attached to any of the animals, but I failed every single time. And being that I watched the doctor try to save Rocky's life, this dog was going to get extra special care from me.

"Come get me when you leave, okay? You were a great help in the surgery," Ken made sure to point out before he stepped free of the gate, leaving the door open.

"Thanks. And I look forward to the brownie."

It took almost an hour for Rocky to wake up from the anesthesia. He was groggy, but instead of seeming confused, he seemed content as I gently ran my hand over the top of his head. Carefully, I extracted myself from beneath him and settled his body against the blankets lying on the floor.

"I'll be back tomorrow," I promised as I closed the door to the run and went in search of Ken and my payment.

Glancing at the clock in the locker room, I was surprised that 4 a.m. was just around the corner. I hurried through a shower and changed my clothes, shoving the dirty ones in my duffle bag. I didn't bother drying my hair, letting the long strands dry naturally.

"I called the rideshare for you," Ken stated as he walked with me out of the building. Ever since the incident on campus, I made it a point to pay for a ride back to the apartment instead of cutting through school. There was still no word on my assailants, but the university police seemed adamant that they didn't go to Wellington. Thank goodness I was able to find my keys in the bushes the next day, but maintenance had already changed the locks. Since then, I made sure that I took more precautions when coming home late at night.

A white sedan pulled up to the curb and Ken greeted the driver while I climbed in the back seat. The ride to the apartment was short and the driver dropped me off just inside the parking lot. After murmuring my thanks and handing her a cash tip, I made my way toward the apartment reaching for the brownie in the front pouch of my duffle bag. My stomach had started growling when I slid from the car and it ferociously announced that it needed sustenance.

I made sure to read the note from Ken's fiancée before tearing into the plastic package.

I love the way you fill out your scrubs.

I couldn't help the grin that inched its way across my face. My heart felt lighter at reading her cute banter and I secretly hoped that one day I'd find someone that I'd be able to toss quick loving jabs.

Opening the door to the apartment stairwell, I almost dropped the sugary goodness as I tried to maneuver my duffle bag through the opening.

"Walk of shame?" a voice called from behind me and I nearly slammed my fingers between the door and the jamb.

I couldn't formulate words as Ford grabbed the door handle and slipped inside. He stared me down in disgust, those eyes that I found mesmerizing looked as if I'd hurt him.

Then his words registered and it was as if a red film curtained over my eyes. I was heated and not in a good way.

Ford tried to walk passed me, but I reached out and gripped his arm, yanking him to face me. I could see that he was already done with this conversation, anxious to get back to his apartment, but I was nowhere near done.

"Excuse me, what did you say?"

"Was it the guy from the café? Did you go back and offer yourself up to him?"

"Oh my gosh, what is your problem?"

Jerking his arm away, Ford began to climb the stairs but I wasn't letting him get away.

"I'm just stating what I saw."

"You saw nothing, you arrogant jerk! And you'd know what a walk of shame is, wouldn't you? Isn't that what you were doing just now?"

I stomped behind him until we reached the third floor. Ford tried to go to his apartment, but I wasn't letting him get away speaking like that to me.

"I was talking to you," I screamed at him as he unlocked his door. I was so angry that I didn't have the chance to feel uncomfortable being back in the apartment. Or the fact that I had followed him into the kitchen where the space was barely big enough for the two of us.

"Are you going to answer me?"

Turning to face me, Ford tossed his keys randomly on the counter and stared me down, his chest heaving with each breath.

"You want to know if I spent the last few hours buried deep in some girl? Want to know how tight her pussy was as she milked my cock? How fast she ripped off the condom so she could suck me off when I came? Is that what you're asking me?"

I couldn't breathe. The air lodged in my lungs, listening to him describe what he had done to some willing female. And I secretly ached that it was me.

He stared at me, waiting for a response, waiting for something. Then I felt that rise growing in me, that he could speak so carelessly in my presence about a woman that had shared herself with him. So now I was furious with her and him.

I took a step closer, bringing my nose just below his chin. The scent I could only describe as Ford's wafted through my senses.

"You're disgusting," I growled at him. "You don't get to know what I do with my time and I certainly have no desire to know about your conquests. Whether or not I spend my night with a random guy will never be any of your business." My voice had risen as I spoke, and somewhere in the back of my mind, I worried that I would wake his brothers, but my exasperation was overflowing and couldn't be stopped.

"It is my business," Ford snarled.

"Why?"

In one quick move, Ford had stepped forward, caging me against the counter, my back pressing against the laminate.

He bellowed, "Because you're mine."

And then we exploded.

Ford crashed his lips against mine before I could react. I was so stunned I stood stock-still as Ford's tongue begged for entrance. My mind had gone numb as I eagerly welcomed him.

He tasted like spearmint and a hint of whiskey. The flavors shouldn't have worked together but I couldn't get enough. Our tongues clashed as I reached my hands around his shoulders. Fistfuls of his cotton shirt crumpled as I clawed at him. I needed to get closer. I needed – more.

Ford seemed to understand my yearning as his strong hands traveled around to the backs of my thighs and lifted me onto the counter. A grunt escaped my lips as my back collided with their coffee maker. Moments later a crash sounded as Ford swiped away the appliance onto the floor before claiming my mouth once again.

We were feverish in our longing to lose ourselves. Our fight for control became a push and pull of our bodies. Those jabs we had tossed back and forth for the last few weeks all led up to this detonation of our desires.

My hands fisted in his hair, those dark locks wedging between my fingers. I gripped at the strands as I lifted my thighs around his waist, using my heels to pull his hips closer to where I needed him most.

I was burning for him, my skin blistered beneath his touch as his fingertips skimmed across my lower back. One moment I was in charge, tilting his head how I wanted, jerking his hips how I needed. Then I felt his hands greedily climb up my back, gathering my shirt as he went. He pulled back from our kiss and I instantly missed the connection, missed his taste. I watched as the corner of his swollen lips tilted upward and I was mesmerized by the motion. On one forceful tug, Ford yanked my shirt over my head and tossed the material blindly to his left.

His stare lasted only a beat until he launched himself toward me. Our teeth clanged as he possessed my mouth, our tongues sliding across each other like a flirtatious dance.

His rough hand slid up the side of my exposed stomach, his calloused fingers leaving a trail of heat as they glided up each individual rib until he reached my jawline. Possessively he cupped my chin, with just enough pressure to maintain control but not enough to hurt me. He titled my head and trailed his kisses from my lips to the top of my throat.

"Ford," I whispered as I leaned back slightly, my head knocking against one of the cupboards.

"Did he kiss you like this?"

What?

It took me a minute to realize what Ford had asked, but he left me no chance to answer as he used his other hand to reach between my legs, the denim doing little to mask the heat I knew he would feel.

"I bet if I slipped my hand beneath your panties, I'd find you soaking wet, wouldn't I, Jolee?" he murmured, his teeth skimming across my soft skin. Despite my anger at his insinuation, I was too far gone to stop. "Did he make you wet like this?"

Ford's palm rubbed up and down my denim-covered center and it took everything in me to keep from leaning back and letting him ravage me.

I may not have had much experience, but I knew what would drive Ford over the edge. I knew what would make him lose control. Even with his lips against my neck and his hand rubbing the place that severely craved his attention, I gathered as much of my wits about me as I could. I barely had enough sense to formulate words as I reached for the back of his head, gripped his hair, and as much as I hated to pull his lips away from my skin, I wanted them back on my mouth.

My other hand reached for his chest, trailing down the hills and valleys of his abdominal muscles, and though they hid behind his long-sleeved Henley, he jolted at my touch. There was no fighting against my smile.

With deft fingers, I flicked at the button of his pants and slithered my hand beneath the elastic waist of his boxer briefs. I didn't have to search hard for his erection, the hardness strained against the confines of his pants. Ford hissed as I softly brushed my finger across the tip of his cock before I spread my fingers and gripped him fully.

"Tell me. Did she touch you like this?" I asked as I nipped at his lower lip. His eyes were closed as he focused on the feel of my stroke. "Did she have her hand wrapped around your cock like this?"

He only allowed himself to get lost in the feeling for a moment. Ford's breath was shallow and shaky as I continued my slow, measured movements while gently nipping his lip, brushing my tongue against it after every bite.

It didn't take long for his control to snap. Ford's eyes popped open and the flicker of a flame shown in those icy blue irises of his.

"You're playing with fire, princess," he bellowed. He probably expected me to stop and cower away, but he should have known better by now. I knew how to act out this scene with him, we'd been rehearsing it for weeks.

"If you can't handle it, I'm sure I can find someone who can finish the job."

And that was the truth. Not that I needed a real person, but my trusty vibrator would get the job done. But I'm sure Ford assumed I meant the fictional person he created in his own mind.

Instantly Ford's mouth was on mine again, savoring every inch of my mouth, and I was lost to him. I had never felt so out of sync with myself – wanting him one minute, hating him the next. There was nothing I could do to control it. There was a hunger for him that wouldn't subside.

For a second, I grew weightless as he lifted me off the counter, my legs wrapped around him as if they had done it a thousand times.

Our kisses grew fiery as he carried me out of the kitchen, the subtle rocking of my body with each step ground his erection against my center. My panties were a lost cause at this point.

We'd only made it about ten steps before Ford turned and pushed my back against the wall. "Fuck, I need to see you," he growled as he released my legs from around his waist, holding me as I placed each leg on the floor.

Blindly he unbuttoned my jeans and my stomach clenched as the backs of his fingers caressed the soft skin just above my panties. My senses swirled as he twisted my body around, my chest and hands pressed against the wall. I watched as a few posters in their frames rattled against the drywall until my eyes sealed with the first press of Ford's lips to the top of my spine. I had never been so glad to shower and change before leaving the animal shelter until this moment, but as he followed every vertebra down my back, every conscious thought left my mind. I could only feel Ford, not just his lips, but the connection. How could we have both ignored it for so long? Is this what Link, Sarah, and Keeley were trying to point out?

With a vigorous tug, Ford wrenched my jeans down to my knees, leaving me both exposed and confined to my clothes. If it were anyone else, I would have squirmed under his stare, but the way Ford's hands stroked against my lace-covered bottom so reverently left me in a state of bliss. His touch was a mixture of gentle and forceful, squeezing with his entire hand, then rubbing his thumb over the same area. I had always been a bit larger than other women in the backside area, for no other reason that I enjoyed carbs and deadlifts at the gym, and it seemed Ford appreciated the effort.

I yelped when he bit the exposed skin of one globe, his teeth pinching at the soft and sensitive skin. Electric sparks flew across my nerve endings. He nibbled again, but my focus turned to his other hand trailing across my upper thigh to my panty covered center. I was so turned on my body shook in need, and if I didn't have some sort of relief soon, I was afraid of what I'd be willing to do.

"Tell me, princess," he began as he slipped one digit beneath my cotton panties. My moan echoed around us as he trailed back and forth against my soaking wet folds. My body was turning into a quivering mess just from the slightest touch from him. "Did he make you wet like this?"

I jerked against his hand, but not in pleasure, except Ford kept a firm grip on my hip to keep me in place as he continued to explore my most sensitive area.

"I think you've only ever been this wet for me. That no man has ever been able to get your body this worked up before."

I wanted to tell him to get off. I wanted to tell him to stop touching me. But I couldn't do either of those things because he wasn't wrong. He had been the only one to work my body into this frenzied state with just a single touch and I worried that I'd never feel anything like this again.

When I didn't respond, he pulled his hand free and a small whimper escaped my lips. "Ford, I. . ." I started to say until he twisted me back around.

His hands rested on the waistband of my jeans which were still dangling at my knees. "Step out," he commanded and I obeyed like one of his many lemmings. By the heat in his eyes as he stared up at me, I knew that there was no point in arguing.

I stood before him clad in only my lace bra and panties I grabbed from a cheap site online, but Ford looked at me as if I was wearing the most exquisite lingerie from France or Spain and he wanted nothing more than to tear it to shreds. Kneeling in front of me, he slid his hands on either side of my hips, the tips of his fingers slipping just beyond the elastic to feel the skin beneath. He was a wolf deciding which delicate piece of flesh to devour first.

And I knew without a doubt that there was absolutely no turning back now, for either of us.

CHAPTER EIGHT

FORD

I didn't know where to start as this goddess stood before me in her pale pink underwear and bra. There was so much for me to look at, so much for me to take in. I wanted to put my mouth on every inch of skin, touch every smooth surface, but I was restless.

Leaning forward, I brushed my nose across the soft material, inhaling her feminine scent. She didn't smell like another man's sex, but I was still furious at the thought that someone had had his hands on her.

My hands again reached for the globes of her ass, the perfect mounds filling my palms as I pushed her hips closer to my face. As much as I wanted to keep my sole focus on her, I couldn't rid my mind of the thoughts that she had been with another man. Every kiss and nip I etched on her stomach marked her as mine.

She was writhing in my arms and I itched to command her every whim. I had never been an alpha in bed, wanting to share the give and take with my partner, but something about Jolee possessed me. I wanted to erase every man she had been with before.

Standing, I pressed my hips against her, the head of my cock rubbing against the skin of her stomach. I didn't correct her when she assumed where I had been. My walk of shame was on the brotherly side, though I had left a willing woman's bed when Tracy had called. The fighting between me and Jolee was like a complicated dance and only we knew the steps to take. The crescendo of the music was building and we weren't immune to its powerful waves.

Reaching up my hand drew down the cup of her bra, exposing a flawless breast and puckered pink nipple. My eyes honed in on that tight peak as I leaned down to taste the sweet perfection. I laved the skin around the areola with my tongue, her hand now lodged in my hair, urging me on. With my other hand, I blindly pulled her other breast free from its confines, gently squeezing the supple skin and rubbing her nipple with my thumb.

"Ungh," she grunted as I pulled my mouth away from the one breast to give my attention to the other.

Her hips swiveled back and forth as she rubbed her thighs together. I was falling into the abyss of pleasuring her, but I knew that I needed to get my head on straight, or I'd lose myself to her completely.

Removing my lips from her breasts, I sealed our mouths together, the kiss wild and untamed. She tangled her hand in my hair, gripping the strands between her delicate fingers. Her slickened breasts pressed against my chest as I gripped the back of her thighs and wrapped them around my hips. My cock jumped as it came in contact with her hot sex as I swallowed her responsive moan.

Using the new leverage and my solid grip I rocked my hips against her, my fingers tightening their grasp as she pried her lips from mine.

Against her neck, I groaned. "I bet I could slide my cock into that tight pussy of yours and you wouldn't stop me, would you?"

She had been so lost in her body's blissful state that I didn't expect to feel her nails grip at my scalp. She tugged my head back and tilted it to the side, licking up the side of my neck to my ear.

"Then you better put on a condom because I don't want to be anywhere near the filth that you've been with," she lamented before sinking her teeth into my ear lobe.

Fuck, that nibble did me in. I released one of my holds on her ass and slammed my hand against the wall as my knees almost buckled. I'd never felt shockwaves like that from a simple bite. Thank goodness she had her legs securely wrapped around my waist or she was at a real risk of falling.

"Back pocket," I groaned, hoping like hell she could figure out a way to reach it.

"Stop talking," Jolee demanded before she crashed her mouth against mine once more. My fingers tried to clutch at the wall, then I remembered it was covered in a textured plaster that was probably tearing up her back from rubbing against it.

Even though my cock was nicely settled between the warmth of her thighs, I made the agonizing journey toward my bedroom. Jolee protested by scraping her teeth against my lower lip but soothed the ache with her tongue. My shins hit the edge of my bed and I reluctantly dropped Jolee from my arms.

I'd expected her to giggle or scowl when she fell onto the mattress, but in typical Jolee fashion, she hinged forward and gripped the top of my pants. I reached into my back pocket and pulled out my wallet and the condom, tossing both onto the middle of the bed, then gripped the cotton of my shirt from between my shoulder blades and pulled it over my head.

My gaze collided with Jolee's as she stared at me reverently. It was a look I had never seen on her before.

"Dang, you're freaking hot," she growled with a subtle lick of her lips. I lifted my hand to trace her tongue's path against her plump mouth, noticing how her eyes dilated at my touch. "Now, take off your pants."

Following her demand, I toed off my shoes and yanked down my pants, boxers and all, in one swoop.

"Of course," she said with her hand in the air, her palm facing toward the ceiling as she gestured to my body. I was fucking proud of the way that I looked and women in the past didn't ever seem to mind. "You have to look like freaking perfection. It's not even fair."

"Are you done?" I asked, eager to get my hands back on her.

She shook her head, her stare leaving a trail of heat across my skin.

My sanity wasn't going to last much longer. "Well, you are now." Bent at the waist, I leaned over her until it forced her to lay back on the bed. My arm wedged between her and the mattress, then I tugged her further on the bed, crawling above her body as we moved. My fingers unhooked her bra and slid one of the straps down her arm and then yanked the material down the other, tossing it aimlessly into my room. Each of her breasts draped to the side and my need to sample them again drove through me. I leaned forward, suckling at the delicate skin a shade lighter than her arms, swirling my tongue around the pink tips.

The pressure from her heels pushed against my ass, urging me closer, but I had other ideas wanting to make her delirious in need. I slipped one of my hands between our bodies, stroking the soaked material of her panties on the outside once, and then twice, then I pushed the material aside and rubbed the slick skin of her folds. The heat emanating from her scorched my fingers but I couldn't pull back, my only desire was to feel the inside of her core. I needed to make sure that she was ready for me, assuming the asshole that she had been with earlier had a small dick.

Fuck, just thinking about another man giving her pleasure had me considering driving home bareback. But as I slipped one finger into her tight sheath and then another, I knew that my assumptions had been wrong. Her tightness gripped me firmer than a fucking Chinese finger trap and I knew that it had been a while since she had been with any man. At least a man worthy of her.

I tried to pull my hand away and revaluate what we were doing, but Jolee's hand gripped my wrist and held my hand against her sex and clit.

"If you pull your hand away before getting me off, I swear I will kill you while you sleep," she seethed and, damn it, it only turned me on more. I loved this vicious side of her. The days where I could rile her up were some of my favorites.

With my thumb, I flicked her swollen clit, watching as her head fell back against the pillows and she closed her eyelids.

Within her channel, I felt her walls begin to quiver as I continued to massage her tight pink pearl. Jolee's legs clamped around my waist as her orgasm hit and I was hypnotized by the puckering of her mouth. My need to claim her became overwhelming and before she finished her release, I had stripped her bare of her underwear and covered myself with the condom.

I sat back on my heels as I aligned my cock at her entrance that was plump and wet and signaling me forward. My gaze drifted up to hers for a moment, silently asking her if this was what she wanted because regardless of all of our bickering and heated foreplay, I would never do something to her that she didn't want. The hand that was resting beside her head reached out and gripped my ass, pulling me closer.

I definitely took that as a yes.

Inch by agonizing inch, I slid my cock inside her sex. My body quaked as I held back from thrusting all the way inside as deep as she could take me. I knew she needed some time to adjust and stretch, but I was barely hanging on, and as I filled her up completely, I could feel the sweat begin to bead along my back.

I never had, in all of my sexual years, felt anything like this sweet heaven my cock had buried itself in.

Rocking my hips back, I plunged forward until I was buried to the hilt. My hand slammed against the wall above her head as I plunged in and out of her core. The sound of the headboard boomed in the room as it clanged over and over into the wall. I was certain to have a dent or hole from the damage we were causing, but nothing could have pulled me away from her at this moment.

I was taken off guard when Jolee's hand pressed against my chest and pushed me back.

Had I hurt her?

But she continued to shove at my shoulder until I was lying flat on my back, sideways on my bed. Jolee lifted one toned leg over my hips until she hovered over my body, my cock seeking out her warmth. A delicate hand reached down and brought my dick in line with her slit and slowly she impaled herself on my erection. Her body settled on top of mine, not moving for a moment, then she leaned forward and placed those pale hands on my chest. Jolee rocked her pelvis up and down in short quick movements, her short nails clawing at my chest, and I had never wanted to tattoo half-moon shapes across my pectorals until then. I'd wear those markings with pride.

Then she did something I didn't expect. Shifting her body so that she was fully seated on me, Jolee swirled those fucking beautiful hips around my shaft and I was gone. My hands flanked either side of her small waist as I held her body in place. I pistoned my hips up and down into her passage, over and over again as I worked to bring us closer to that crest. I watched enraptured as my cock coated in her honey with every thrust, and at Jolee's moan, I pulled my eyes away and glanced at her. It was fucking torture, but I was gloriously rewarded as I watched a drop of sweat trail from between her breasts down to the divot of her navel. I was fascinated by its movement until my attention was captured by Jolee's hand sliding across her mound, heading straight for her clit. She looked like a god damn vision leaning back with one hand on my shin and the other swirling around her bundle of nerves. My release was skyrocketing closer and I needed to make sure that Jolee got hers.

Thankfully her walls chose that moment to squeeze the life out of my cock as she plummeted over the edge toward her climax. Her body stiffened in my hands as I increased the speed of my thrusts. The tingling in my spine was the first indication that my release was near. I sat up and gripped the back of Jolee's head, plunging my tongue into her mouth as I expelled myself into the latex.

Together we fell back against the bed, my arms wrapping around her shoulders so that she landed firmly on my chest, my cock slipping free from her heat. Our breaths moved in unison and I was worried at how right, at how perfect it felt to be lying here with Jolee after the craziest bout of sex of my life. I wanted to ask her if it was okay. For some reason her feelings actually mattered and I wasn't clamoring for my clothes and a reason to leave.

She must have sensed my change in thought because without moving her sated body, she said, "If you start talking, I'm going to bite your nipple." Of course, she made sure to prove her point further by licking the tip of my nipple, sending a shiver down my spine.

"Who's to say I wouldn't like it?" I replied.

"Masochist."

I chuckled as I reluctantly removed myself from beneath her body. "I need to take care of the condom."

"Okay," she whispered, lying on her stomach, her head barely hanging off the edge of my bed.

On wobbly legs, I walked over to the trash can beside my desk, pulled the condom off, and tossed it in the bin. When I turn around, I took in her naked body and leaned back against my desk. She had perfect curves and an ass that I couldn't wait to sink my teeth into. And as my erection began to stiffen between my legs, it seemed as if my cock had the same consideration.

"I can feel you staring at me."

"Hard not to," I replied as I made my way back toward her. I laid on the bed and, though she resisted at first, I tugged her over to me. Jolee laid her head on my chest and a leg across my thigh. The difference in our skin was alluring – her pallor to my bronze. She had a freckle on her exposed shoulder and I found myself enamored by the small mutation on her skin. I reached across with my hand and ran my fingers through her thick waves, surprised at the softness as they slipped between my digits.

Her breathing became shallow as I continued the strokes and I was convinced she had fallen asleep. I was surprised at myself for not kicking her out of my bed. But once I slowed my massage, she whispered in a gravelly voice, "If you stop, I will kill you."

Jolee's head bobbed as I chuckled and I earned myself a tweak of my nipple by my sadistic companion. "Why so violent?"

"I'd hate for you to know that I'm comfortable right now, but it's the truth."

"Worried I'd use it to my advantage?" I inquired as I glided my hand from her hair down the side of her hips and gripped a generous amount of her ass.

In response, Jolee crossed both her arms and perched them on my chest, her brown eyes piercing me with their stare. I felt like I was seeing her for the first time. The light from the outside of the apartment illuminated the room and there was nothing more beautiful than Jolee's body illuminated by the orange glow.

"You weren't with another guy tonight, were you?" I asked and she shook her head, some of the blonde strands of hair falling down our sides, tickling my ribs.

"I was at the animal shelter volunteering. We had a late case come in and I was asked to stay."

"So, no guy?"

"Only one of the black Labrador persuasion. What about you? What lucky female had their chance at the great rogue himself, Ford O'Brien?"

"Well, my mom would say that she's pretty lucky."

"You were at your mom's?" she asked, surprised. Her body jolted at her question.

"Archer and Link came down with the stomach bug and the big babies wanted to be with Tracy, so I was there delivering supplies. I fell asleep on the couch."

A smile slowly crept across her face. I wasn't sure if it was due to the knowledge that we both made assholes of ourselves with our assumptions, or that we just spent the better part of an hour fucking each other senseless.

"I guess I shouldn't feel so bad about all of the noise we caused. I was worried we'd wake them up."

"Archer probably would have grabbed a bowl of popcorn and watched."

She giggled at my joke and I couldn't take being this far away from her anymore. I used my hand to guide her body closer until our lips met. This time we were gentle, explorative, as if we were two young lovers learning each other for the first time. It was the most addictive thing I had ever done – she was going to be my craving.

I wasn't sure how long we stayed there kissing like teenagers, but a monstrous growl sounded from her stomach and ricocheted off the walls.

"Sorry, I missed dinner and you interrupted my lunch."

What the?

"You should have said something. I would have fed you."

Pushing herself off my body, Jolee sat in her nakedness, but I could sense that she wasn't quite comfortable in her skin. Her hair draped over her breasts and she kept her legs tightly pressed together.

"We were a bit busy, Ford."

Damn it, she was right. But there had been so many days I had gone without food as a kid, at no fault of my mothers, but there were nights we didn't have much to survive on. Being hungry isn't something anyone should ever have to experience.

"You're right," I told her, and even in the shadows of the room, I could see her eyebrows jut up in surprise. "Let me make you the Ford breakfast of champions." Standing from the bed I pulled her along with me, my hand clasping hers tightly as I dragged her to the kitchen.

"Does this breakfast come with a side of poison?" she joked with a single brow raised. God, she really was hot when she was in her firecracker mode.

"Nope, not today at least."

Leaving her at the entrance of the kitchen, I walked to the pantry and grabbed a box of my favorite cereal, one that I shared with no one, and placed it on the counter. I quickly added two bowls, two spoons, and the jug of milk to my array then went to making the perfect bowl of cereal.

"Here you go," I said smugly as I set the bowl on the peninsula in front of her.

"You eat Cookie Crisp? What are you? Twelve?"

I stared at her in mock horror then reached back for the bowl which I had bestowed upon her. But she swatted my hand away before I could snatch it away.

"How dare you speak poorly of my snack choice. Cookie Crisp is the perfect late-night food choice. And it was my favorite as a kid. I don't think you're worthy of my cereal."

She was giggling now as I argued my point and it took every ounce of my control not to flick my eyes down to where her breasts lightly jiggled with her laugh.

"I'm sorry," she replied as she took a hearty scoop of cereal and ate it. Her eyes widened in surprise and I shook my head at her reaction. "Wow, these are way better than I remember."

"Told you."

We finished our snack and Jolee helped me rinse the bowls and place them in the dishwasher before standing in my kitchen, looking around nervously.

"So, I guess I should probably find my things."

I took a step closer to her, and then another, my eyes glued to how her chest rose and fell with each breath. The motion grew faster and faster until I was standing right up against her body, then it stopped altogether.

"Why?" I asked as I trailed a finger from the edge of her wrist up her arm and across her shoulder until my hand slid behind the back of her neck.

Breathlessly, Jolee replied, "I figured I'd head upstairs. I thought we were done."

Gripping her hair gently, I forced her head back so that I could lean closer, nipping the corner of her mouth. "We're not done until I say we're done."

Just as before, our lips brushed across each other's as I lifted her in my arms and carried her back to my bedroom.

The problem for me was that I wasn't sure I was ever going to be done with her. And as she fell asleep in my bed with the sun flickering over the horizon, I knew that I was on the verge of doing the one thing I had sworn I wouldn't. I didn't get tied up in women. I didn't let them mess with my mind or my plan. And I knew what I was going to have to do when Jolee woke. I was going to have to turn back into the asshole that I was growing to hate.

The writing on the wall had been there all along through the arguing, the bickering, the side-eyes. I usually deserved most of what she dished out, but it was in retaliation of something I had said or done. She hadn't deserved any of it.

She had no idea the effect she had on men, especially the ones at the school. She was beautiful, strikingly so, and every male I knew on campus hadn't had the courage to approach her. And if they knew how she spent her free time, hell, they'd probably start lining up with engagement rings.

My grip on her hip tightened. I hated the thought of her being with anyone else, but I knew this hot and cold match that she and I played wouldn't last forever. She would grow tired of this game and meet a man that was worthy of her.

But she felt like mine - I wanted her to be mine. But my sperm donor father wasn't a stupid man. I knew he kept tabs on me and if he ever found out that I had an interest in a woman, he would make sure that relationship fizzled out faster than a tablet of Alka-Seltzer.

It wasn't just my plan for revenge that I needed to protect, it was Jolee too. She didn't need to get mixed up in this mess that was my life. There was no mercy where my father was concerned. I actually feared he might do his worst just to spite me.

I worried myself into sleeplessness as Jolee snoozed on my chest, the only movement coming from her was the small up and down motions of her back. I couldn't fathom the things my father was capable of if the leads Brent had were correct.

The sun shined fully into the room and I knew that I didn't have much time left in this peaceful bubble that Jolee and I had created for the night. I stared down at her serene face. The soft slope of her nose, the Cupid's bow of her full upper lip, the small elfish point on the tip of her ears, I was taking it all in. It was probably going to be the last time I was ever this close to her again.

And as much as I wish that I could force her to belong to me, I knew that I was going to have to let her go.

RENEE HARLESS

CHAPTER NINE

JOLEE

The pattering of rain sounded on the window and it kept lulling me in and out of sleep. I wasn't sure of the time, but from the way my body ached, I was convinced that it must be late in the afternoon. Whenever I pulled late nights at the shelter, my body protested the next day.

I turned over on the bed and reached for my body pillow but came up empty-handed. It wasn't often that I moved a lot when I slept, but my limbs must have had some residual energy from the long hours.

"Grumph," I mumbled as I forced my eyes open. My lids were heavy with sleep and exhaustion, and it took longer than normal, but once they were open, I immediately shut them. The chair in the corner and the poster on the wall seemed familiar – except they weren't mine.

Then everything rushed through my mind like a Formula-One car on a track in Europe. My chest heaved as I worked to catch my breath. I was in Ford's room, naked.

Oh goodness, what had I done?

Except I knew the answer to that question, it was quite simple. I gave in. We had been fighting each other for so long that we had built this massive mountain made of emotions and hateful words. It wasn't going to take much to send us careening off the sides into the sea of desire crashing like waves along the edges.

And the splash from the fall was as volatile as the climb.

I watched the rain splatter against the windowpane, the droplets slipping and sliding against each other as they made their descent. I felt like those raindrops, determined to stay on my own path until something collided into me and I was knocked off course. David had been the first and I had sworn that there wouldn't be a chance for another. But I had never planned on Ford.

A car alarm sounded off in the distance and I knew that I had wasted enough time. Closing my eyes, I turned back over on the bed until I was facing the other direction.

One. Two. Three.

Holding my breath, I opened my eyes only to find the other side of the bed empty. I released a heavy sigh, unsure if I was feeling angered or grateful that Ford wasn't lying on the other side of the mattress.

Sitting up in the bed, I gripped the sheet that was draped across my hip and held it against my chest while looking around the room. He had an old wooden desk covered in papers and notebooks and a laptop that was closed. I wasn't one to snoop, but the thought crossed my mind to figure out what made a guy like Ford tick.

Instead, I found myself standing from the bed and wrapping the sheet around my body in that dress-like way women do in the movies. I'd never considered that I would be doing that same stereotypical day-after-sex move.

My bra was dangling precariously off a book stand, but my panties were nowhere to be found. Though, it was doubtful that I'd be wearing those again any time soon.

"Ford?" I called out as I opened the door of his bedroom.

Even though I knew his brothers had spent the night at their mother's house the night before, I was cautious as I took my first step into the hallway.

When Ford didn't answer, I called his name out again. It didn't take long for me to realize that I was completely alone in the apartment. If I hadn't been angry before, I was furious now.

My jeans and shirt from the night before were resting on the arm of the sofa and I stomped my way over to them. Carelessly I dropped the sheet from my grasp, the cotton material pooling on the floor at my feet. Sans undergarments, I tugged on my jeans and pulled the shirt over my head. I only needed to go up one flight of stairs, and frankly, I didn't care if anyone saw me. My breasts were perky enough that I didn't really need a bra beneath my shirt anyway. Ford could hang onto my bra as a memento because that was the closest he would get to seeing my underwear again.

I found my flats and duffle bag in the kitchen and looked out into the apartment. The sheet was lying on the floor and I had to force myself to leave it there. I didn't need to clean up his mess.

The bag felt heavier than I remembered, and as I slipped the strap over my head, I tried not to think of what happened last night. How Ford had lifted me onto the kitchen counter and I had lost control.

"It was a one-time thing," I whispered to myself as if I needed the reminder.

Except somewhere deep inside, I wished it wasn't. It was easy to ignore my attraction to Ford when we were sitting in class, but when we were alone that was a different story. He flipped the switch inside me that I thought I had disabled. No boy was going to have possession of me like that again, it's why I fought so hard against Ford. But in one night, he decimated my walls completely. I just hoped this time it wouldn't take nearly as long to build them back.

I was about to step out of the kitchen when an idea formulated in my mind. An idea that would hit Ford where it really hurt. Opening the pantry, I searched until I found his coveted box of Cookie Crisp. I reached deep inside and pulled out the clear plastic bag then shoved it into the side pocket of my duffle bag. I slipped the box back onto its hidden shelf as if it had never been moved.

Since waking in Ford's bed alone, I smiled wickedly for the first time.

Exiting the apartment, I checked the knob and made sure that their door was locked. I may be angry, but

I wasn't malicious. Just as I turned around, I heard a playful voice call my name.

"Jolee?" Chance said. He eyeballed me and then the apartment door.

"Hi." I was nervous that he'd seen me leaving their apartment. My voice squeaked and my hand jutted upward in an awkward wave.

"Were you just?"

Sighing, I replied," Yeah." There was no point in hiding it where I had been. My ability to think on my feet was lacking.

"But they. . ." His words lingered in the air. Chance didn't need to finish his sentence, I knew what he was implying. It was even worse when his eyes drifted down to the duffle bag resting on my hip.

"Yeah."

"He's not a bad guy, Jolee."

Of course his brother would try to stand up for him – that's what family did. But he couldn't save Ford. I didn't think anyone could.

"He is, but that's okay." I stepped toward the stairs that would take me to the fourth floor. "Have a good day, Chance."

"Yeah, you too," he replied, his voice lower than before.

I tried not to think about Ford's brothers finding out that we slept together the night before. It wasn't their business, but I got a hint of joy knowing that they'd tear into him. I may not know them well, but we all got along the night Link gave me a place to stay.

In record speed, I zoomed through my apartment and straight into the bathroom. I was thankful that neither Willow or Haley were around. But as I started the shower, my need to wash away the night growing with every passing second, a knock sounded on the bathroom door.

"Jolee? Is that you? I've been freaking out not knowing where you were."

I never had girl friends growing up, not ones that knew all of your deepest desires and secrets. And knowing that I may have worried my roommates left a bitter taste in my mouth.

Despite my natural instinct to pack away my emotions into a tightly compressed box, I found myself shouting to Willow, "I'll tell you everything when I get out."

Sitting on the couch between Willow and Haley with a glass of red wine in my hand, I was waiting for their reaction after I divulged everything that had happened with Ford. Willow blinked her large brown eyes that were a trait on my mother's side and Haley stared with her jaw agape. I gave them every sordid detail, assuming that was what girls did when they gossiped, but I may have overindulged.

"Okay," Willow said first, then took a sip of her wine. "That was not what I was expecting. But damn, girl, please tell me he is as good in bed as he looks."

"Gosh, it was so good. I don't know if it was all of the tension between us or what, but I didn't know sex could be so. . . "

I glanced around the room trying to come up with the right word.

"Hot?"

"Amazing?" they both chimed in.

"Explosive."

Haley grabbed the book on the coffee table and fanned herself.

Willow sat her glass on the end table and stood from the couch saying, "I think this calls for a celebration."

"What are we celebrating?" I asked as I watched her move into the kitchen. Willow returned with a second bottle of wine and a cheesecake from her shelf in the fridge.

"Haley," she commanded. "Call in two large pizzas. We need to recognize my cuz Jolee and her accomplishment at bringing Ford to his knees."

"I didn't," I tried to explain as Haley began speaking into her phone and Willow popped the cork to the wine.

"Oh, but you did. It is a widely known fact that Ford never sleeps with a woman in his bed. And he is out the door the moment it's over. He doesn't linger. He doesn't make small talk. And the fact that you stayed the night in his bed, twice I might add, and did the dirty all over his apartment, I'm fairly confident that you, my dear cousin, indeed brought him to his knees."

Rationally I understood what Willow was saying, but regardless of what Ford had done with other women and with me, I just felt that we were back at that stairwell with him giving me the angered stare. I wasn't sure if we were ever going to get past that moment.

"Pizza will be here in ten," Haley stated as she queued up *Coyote Ugly* on the television.

We cuddled on the couch beneath a single blanket as the movie began. When the buzzer rang with our pizza, Haley ran down to pay the delivery boy and she was back in record time.

Raising her glass in the air as we sat with paper plates of pizza on our laps, Willow said, "To Jolee."

Haley repeated the saying and the two chimed their glasses against mine.

It wasn't long before we moved on from the second bottle of wine to the third. It felt good to let loose and enjoy the quiet time with my roommates and not worry about what was going on outside of this moment.

One of the dance sequences began on the screen and before I knew it, Haley had us pulled up on the couch dancing wildly. My body moved with the beat of the song and I closed my eyes as I let the rhythm take me over.

"Dance Party!" Willow shouted as she paused the movie and switched the screen to a music station. Bass pumped through the speakers and vibrated the framed pictures against the walls. I had felt shackled in my life before coming to Wellington, but now there wasn't anything weighing me down. Those iron binds wouldn't get the chance to wrap themselves around my wrists again. This, here with my cousin and friend, dancing wildly in our apartment was more than I could have imagined. My parents didn't think that I was strong enough for this journey, but I was determined to prove them wrong.

The music switched to one of my favorites, a song with a fast beat and thumping lyrics. I reached for the remote and turned up the volume before using the device as a fake microphone. Willow, Haley, and I laughed hysterically, and when Haley jumped off the couch, claiming that she was going to pee herself, our laughs grew louder.

Unexpectedly the door to our apartment flew open. Willow screamed and I jerked my head to stare at our three arrivals in hatred since they single-handedly ruined my celebration.

"Having a party and didn't invite us?" a deep voice asked. I recognized the ridge rogue as Rylan.

"How did you know we were having a party? And how the fuck did you get inside?" Haley asked as she walked out of the hall. I started laughing again at her shocked expression. There was a whole lot of gorgeous standing in our doorway.

Chance chose that moment to speak up as Rylan was staring down Haley.

"The door was unlocked."

"Just because the door was unlocked doesn't mean you should barge in," I said, my hands planted firmly on my hips. "And furthermore," my gaze traveled to Ford who was standing behind Rylan and Chance as if he'd rather be anywhere else, "you're not wanted." Their attention on me only seemed to rise me up even more. Stepping off the couch, I moved onto the coffee table, using it as a pedestal for my tirade. From the corner of my eye, I watched as Willow reached out to me, but I had a point to make. "I know you rogues think that you're better than everyone else, but-" The table wobbled beneath my feet, and before I could react, the top broke free from the wobbly table leg Willow had warned me about over and over again. It took just a second before I was staring at the ceiling instead of the gorgeous faces of the ridge rogues.

Shouts and cries rang through the room as I fixated my eyes on a cobweb in the corner.

"Jolee!"

"Are you okay?" Willow and Haley asked. I had hoped that they would reach me first, but I wasn't surprised to see Ford's exasperating face hovering over mine. The same hands that had explored every inch of my body the night before cupped the back of my head.

"Are you hurt anywhere?"

I drew my gaze from the ceiling and watched as he took in my body from the tips of my toes to the top of my head.

"I. . .I'm fine."

"How many fingers am I holding up?" he questioned only to receive a rolling of my eyes in response.

"Go away, Ford," I murmured as I moved to sit up, my back aching in protest with the motion. He kept his hand on the back of my neck and I swatted it away, glaring at him. Did he not understand that I wanted nothing to do with him?

He held his hands up in surrender and turned away. "Let's go," he told his brothers. Chance followed closely behind, but Rylan lingered for a moment before turning his eyes away from Haley.

"Lock the door," he growled to us before slamming it after their retreat.

"Oh. My. God." Willow punctuated each word as she spoke.

"I'm sorry I broke the table."

"I couldn't care less about the table. But, oh my gosh, Jolee. Ford got to you so fast it made my head spin. And you should have seen the look on his face."

I was busy gathering our wineglasses and the pizza boxes, but I glanced at Willow and Haley over my shoulder, noticing that Haley still had a glazed look on her face.

"What kind of look did he have?" I asked, my curiosity getting the better of me.

"He looked. . .I don't know. Like he would murder anyone if a single hair on your head was harmed, but he looked distraught too. I can't really describe it other than it's not an expression I've ever seen him wear around campus."

"You're delusional." Setting the glasses in the sink, I glanced up to Haley, who was nodding her head.

"I saw him too," she said as she walked toward me. "And believe me, I don't think they would have rushed up here if it was just Willow and me."

"Even if that's the case, Ford and I. . .it was just a one-time thing. And really, I can't wait for this semester to be over so I don't have to prepare myself for battle against him every other day." Angrily I folded up the cardboard boxes and shoved them into our recycling bin then turned back to my friends. "Thank you, guys, for tonight. It was fun. But I think I'm going to go catch up on some sleep."

We said our goodnights and I went into my bedroom, collapsing on the mattress. The soft bounce of my body reminded me of the way that Ford had tossed me on his bed.

Was I destined to have things remind me of that night for my entire life?

There was one thing for sure though, it was a night that I was likely never to forget anytime soon.

Since the sleepover at Ford's, my schedule had been thrown for a loop. The nights I laid awake in bed until the sun began to rise only to find myself fighting off the exhaustion while I was at class and work.

My eyelids had just started closing when a knock on my bedroom door sounded.

"Jolee, girl, you're going to be late to class."

"Son of a beach!" I shouted as I hopped off the bed. Wildly I pulled clothes from my dresser, opting for a pair of black pants and a red long-sleeved shirt. I ripped off my pajamas and tugged on my pants, hopping around like a rabbit until I lost my footing and fell face-first into my desk chair. It was going to leave a mark, but I didn't care.

I needed to be in class today. Not just to throw comments at Ford, but because our midterm was next week and today was the first review session.

My hands gripped the cotton of my shirt and I yanked it over my head, then I shoved my arms through the sleeves, all while walking into the bathroom to brush my teeth. There would be no time for makeup today.

I was zipping up my boots and sliding my bag over my shoulder as I met Haley and Willow at the door.

"Thanks for waiting," I told them.

"Still not sleeping?" Willow asked as we jogged down the steps and I shook my head.

I'd barely slept a total of ten hours in the two weeks since Ford ruined sleep forever. I just needed to get through to next week when we had Thanksgiving break. Flying back to Alaska was out of the question and my parents were going to be off doing more research. I planned to stay at the apartment and do absolutely nothing for four days straight.

The girls and I parted at the fountain in the center of campus, just as we had that first day of classes. The sun was shining brightly on the school grounds, but the forecast was calling for rain the rest of the week. Something I was not looking forward to. I could deal with the cold, but rain and I didn't mesh well together.

Grabbing my phone from my pocket, I glanced at the time and my breath whooshed from my lungs in relief because I was arriving earlier than normal.

I opened the door to the lecture hall and to my surprise there sat the tortuous man in my chair. A smug smile grew on Ford's face as I walked over to my row. He probably assumed that I would take the seat he usually occupied, but I wasn't going to let Ford throw my day off track. I was lucky enough that I hadn't overslept, I didn't need him to cast a new halo of gloom over me.

"Good morning." I smiled brightly at him as I slipped passed, arching my back ever so slightly so that my backside was closer to him than was necessary.

"What are you doing?" he asked, baring his clenched teeth at me as I sat in the chair next to him.

"Well, I like my seat, and I also like to sit next to Keeley and Sarah. And since you took the seat I usually occupy, I simply moved over one. Does it bother you to be so close to me, Ford?"

"No."

"Good, because I'm going to pretend that you don't exist at all," I told him as the rest of the class filed in. I could see in the way his hand tensed on the edge of the desk that I had hit a nerve. Luckily the professor chose that moment to enter the room and I was saved from Ford's backlash at least for the moment. There was no telling what he was capable of.

That evening the girls and I planned a night out. Nothing crazy because we weren't the partying kind, all three of us preferred to spend our time studying in the library or binge-watching shows. Tonight was Willow's choice for dinner and she had heard rumblings of a pub off campus that had great food and atmosphere.

"It's where the locals go. My organic chemistry lab partner is from the area and says that it's the best."

It sounded good to me, but I was worried that we'd walk in and everyone would turn in their seats to stare at the newcomers. "Are you sure that we won't, you know, stand out?"

"No, she said college students drop in all the time. But it's not like, a college restaurant, you know?"

Haley and Willow both wore similar outfits of jeans, gray sweaters, and black boots. I opted for my red pants and cream-colored sweater with my brown boots that just skimmed beyond my knees.

Willow curled my hair into soft waves that ran down my back and I kept my makeup light and easy. I wasn't going there to impress anyone. Sitting in economics with Ford's scent swirling around me the entire class, I kept telling myself that a boy wasn't in my plan. I needed to remember that falling for someone wasn't going to help rescue animals. Even though I really wanted to lean closer to the man that left me in the morning light alone in his bed, I had to force myself to maintain my distance.

"The rideshare is waiting. Are you guys ready?" Haley asked, peeking her head into my bedroom. Her dark hair was pulled back into a sleek ponytail.

"Yeah," Willow and I said in unison as we exited my bedroom.

The car ride took us about thirty minutes from the school toward an area filled with large, stately homes. I began to question if we were going in the right area until the car stopped outside of a small brick building that looked as if it had been converted into a restaurant.

"This is it."

From the back seat, I handed the driver a tip since it was my turn to pay and exited the car behind Haley. It felt like we were intruding as we followed Willow to the back side of the building, where a few people in heavy coats gathered at a table beneath a heat lamp. I spied glasses filled with some type of beer and assumed we had made it to a pub of some sort.

"Come on," Willow called out to me as she gestured for me to follow them to the door. I hadn't realized that I had stopped moving as I took in the group.

"My lab partner said her brother was working as a server tonight and we could request his section."

Something felt off as we stepped inside the pub. There was a woman standing at the entrance with intricate tattoos snaking up her arms and I immediately wanted to get a better look at them. She and Willow spoke for a minute and then she directed us over to an empty booth along the far wall.

A few patrons glanced up from their meals and drinks, but no one paid us any mind, just as Willow had promised. We each grabbed one of the laminated menus on the table and our eyes widened at the selection. This pub didn't serve your typical fried foods and burgers. No, this menu had five-star meals.

Tuna tartare. Filet mignon with Hollandaise sauce. Duck confit. Lamb ragu with pasta.

My mouth watered as I read through the selections.

"Surprised?" Willow asked as she peered at us over her menu.

"Very," Haley replied and I nodded. I wasn't sure that I could afford the meals here, but I was certainly impressed.

I trained my eyes to stay on their salad selection because they were the only compilations that were in my budget.

A soft hand reached out from across the table and rested on mine as it held the menu in its grasp. "Jolee, this one is on me." I blinked as Willow spoke. "Please, let me do this for you."

"You've helped me out so much. And I still owe you for the table."

"Oh, be quiet, you do not owe me for the table. And besides, this is what friends and family do."

I sat the menu down and glanced through watery eyes at my cousin. "I haven't really had either before."

"I know, and we're changing that. So, let me buy your dinner. Victoria, my lab partner, says that the duck is to die for."

Her friend's brother stopped by the table and took our drink and food orders. He was cute and couldn't seem to take his eyes off Willow. I had a sneaking suspicion that Victoria had been masterminding a love connection.

"Have you heard from your parents recently?" Willow asked as our meals were placed in front of us. The duck confit looked and smelled delicious and I couldn't wait to sink my teeth into it, but Willow's mentioning of my parents turned my stomach sour.

Before I answered her, I made sure to take a bite of the duck before I completely lost my appetite. I didn't discuss my family much, if at all. They hadn't wanted me to leave Alaska, but they barely spent any time with me while I was there. It was their way of controlling a situation, which for two people that were free spirits and nonconformists, they had no idea what they were doing.

"I spoke to them after fall break. That was the last time. They were headed to another mountain range with a new research team."

Willow took a small bite of her filet and chewed the delicate meat daintily as she considered my words. "Are they still investigating the-"

"Stop," I interrupted. I didn't like anyone to know what my crazy parents examined. They spent all of their time researching and creating new theories, but most of the people in our town thought my parents were nuts.

"What do they investigate?" Haley asked, not wanting to be left out.

I sighed and set down my fork. Blindly I reached into my purse and grabbed my phone, typing Japan Flight 1628 into the browser and handed it to Haley.

"Oh! Wow, so they research. . ."

Holding up my hand, I beg her not to continue. "Please don't say it."

"I just. . .I didn't know that it was a thing."

"Oh, it definitely is. There is an entire community of people obsessed. Now, can we please talk about something else?"

We switched topics to our plans for Thanksgiving. Willow and her family were going down to Florida to visit her other grandmother, while Haley was traveling home to be with her parents. They both wanted me to join them, but I was looking forward to the downtime alone.

We were on our third drink, Haley's courtesy of her fake ID, when the air in the room shifted. Haley's eyes widened and it seemed I wasn't the only one to notice. With a shaking hand, I put my mojito back on the table and turned toward the door where the ridge rogues walked in as if they owned the place. And as they bypassed the crowd waiting for a table, it seemed that maybe they did.

A statuesque woman with a short gray haircut walked behind them, smiling and waving at the servers and a few patrons as she passed. As they passed our table, I breathed a sigh of relief, assuming that we had gone unnoticed. But I should have known better.

The boys stood to the side as they let the women slide into the center of the rounded booth, then they each piled in beside her—three on one side and three on the other. Four of the guys immediately lifted their menus and began shouting back and forth about what they were going to eat while the other two stared directly at our table – Ford and Rylan.

I didn't know what was going on with Rylan and Haley, but I could feel Ford's intense scolding stare across the room. It practically burned my skin. We were invading their space and they weren't pleased about it.

"Willow, I think we should go."

"No, we can eat here too. Don't let him kick us out."

My saucy cousin had a point, and truthfully she always seemed so turned into herself that I was surprised she had wanted to go out into a crowded space at all. I remembered how meek she seemed at the airport picking me up, but I've come to know that Willow was anything but meek. And after a few drinks, she seemed to let her hair down.

Luckily, Haley agreed with my desire to leave and we overruled Willow. She huffed and pouted as we paid the bill. The rideshare was close by so we filed out of the booth and made our way to the exit. Something tugged at me deep in my chest and I couldn't help but turn around and look back at the booth where Ford sat. His brows furrowed, only highlighting those blue eyes that struck me so many weeks ago. The same blue eyes that were both pleading with me to stay and begging me to go. With a gentle pull on my arm, I pried my eyes away from him and continued following my roommates out of the pub. But, somehow, it felt like I had left a piece of myself behind.

RENEE HARLESS

CHAPTER TEN

FORD

I sat in Jolee's chair in our economics class for the third time and patiently waited for her to arrive. Today was our last review session before midterms and I was only there to get a rise out of her, I could pass an entry-level economics class with flying colors for no other reason than I studied the textbook over the summer.

Students had their assumptions about me: I was broody, angry, trouble. But what they failed to catch or try to learn was that I was smart too. All the free time I spent outside of school was done studying. I masked my brains with black and leather, barely giving anyone the chance to learn that part of me. I had a feeling Jolee suspected, though. She had commented more than once that I wasn't taking notes and that the material was important. I only responded with a smirk and flicked at a key or two on her computer.

I waited patiently for her to walk into the lecture hall, remembering how stunning she had looked in those damn red pants last Monday when we were at Tracy's friend's pub. I couldn't pull my gaze from her until she left. Even then I was lost in my own world, remembering how my heartbeat had stopped when I watched her fall from their coffee table. Tracy had begun to pry and my brothers made sure to point out that she was the woman that had me tied up in knots. They still had no idea that we had slept together, even though Chance kept giving me weird glances.

Jolee's two friends hurried into the classroom, quickly followed by the professor, and I immediately sat up in my seat. She had never missed a class. Never even came close to missing the door locking.

I turned to look at the girl whose name I thought was Keeley and asked, "Do you know where Jolee is?"

Her eyes grew in size at my question, probably because I had never spoken a word to anyone in class besides Jolee. "I'll. . .uh. . .send her a text."

That wasn't nearly enough, but it was going to have to do.

My knee bounced up and down the entire lecture until the class dismissal. Jolee had never returned Keeley's message which had my anxiety skyrocketing. Dashing from the classroom and out of the building, I sprinted around crowds of students, moving quickly between them on my way back to the apartment.

Thank goodness for my daily five-mile runs because I had barely broken a sweat as I reached the fourth floor, having taken the steps two at a time. My fist pounded against the door as I called out her name, but when there was no response, I twisted the doorknob. Panic surged through me like electricity as I opened the unlocked door. My eyes and ears searched the place but nothing seemed to be amiss, at least from what I remembered when I was here last.

I made my way down the hall, opening every door on my way, finding them empty. I knew neither of the bedrooms were Jolee's – they didn't look like her personality at all. One was full of music posters while the other was full of flowers and twinkling lights. At the final door at the end of the hall, the bedroom a floor above mine, I twisted the cold metal knob.

Taking a deep breath, I opened it slightly to peek inside, there she was.

And I had never been more furious in my life.

"Jolee," I growled, but the small vixen with her bare backside turned toward me, the sweet flesh peeking out from beneath the sheet, moaned in reply.

"Jolee!" I repeated, my voice raised as my body grew in awareness of her naked state.

"Huh? Ford?" she asked as she turned on her stomach and faced me. Her eyes were heavy with sleep as she blinked in confusion.

"Are you sick?"

Jolee's pink tongue peeked out and licked at her dry lips and I had to stifle a groan that was building in my gut.

"No. . ." she said as she sat up, the sheet slipping down to her waist.

I needed to get out of there. Being so close to Jolee's perfect body and knowing that I couldn't touch it was sweet torture that was growing by the second. My fingers twitched against my thighs wanting to touch her. Closing my eyes, I took a deep breath trying to calm myself, but that only added to my agony as her scent swirled around me. I couldn't have imagined a sweeter hell than this moment.

I had to leave. Blindly I reached into my bag and took out the notebook I scribbled the lecture onto and held it out for her to take.

"Wha-"

"Take it."

When the paper slipped from my hand into hers, I turned on my heels and made a beeline for the exit. My chest was heavy, as if I was having a panic attack.

"Ford?" she called out and I wanted to ignore her beckoning, tried with everything that I was, but I paused with my hand resting on the doorknob of her apartment. I could hear the soft patter of her feet coming down the hallway and found myself exhaling a deep breath. My body was geared up for a fight, and this time I wasn't sure that it would be against Jolee, it was going to be against myself.

"Are these. . .are these your notes from class?"

"It's no big deal." Except it was. It's not something that I would have done for anyone else except her. I knew that school was important to her and I knew she'd hate herself if she missed something right before the midterm.

"Ford, look at me, please." Her voice was so soft, so reverent, and even though I knew better, I found myself releasing the doorknob and turning to face her. Jolee had her sheet wrapped around her body like a dress and I wondered for a moment if that was how she had worn my navy sheet when I had left her in my bed. She appeared like an ethereal goddess in front of me and I was severely lacking to be in her presence.

"Thank you. I don't know how I can repay you for this."

"Like I said, it's no big deal."

One elegant leg peeked out from behind the slit in the sheet as she took a step toward me. It had been an agonizing few days knowing how I left things with her and if she touched me, I was going to ravage her like a caged animal.

"But it is a big deal. You don't even take notes in class. I'm intrigued to know why."

"Stop, Jolee. Just take the notes, or don't. It doesn't matter to me."

"Really? Then why are you here, Ford? Why not just let me suffer? I could have asked Keeley or Sarah for their notes."

Her skin was turning the prettiest shade of pink as she raised her voice and I watched in fascination as that color crept up from her chest to her cheeks.

"You're looking too far into this. I tried to do something nice, obviously it's not something that I'll do again anytime soon."

"You're ignoring my question."

Crossing my arms against my chest, the tension between us was growing as she grew more irritated. We were engaged in verbal warfare and it was delightful.

"What question was that?" I asked with a single corner of my lips tilting upward in a smirk. Her eyes blinked as she watched the grin move upward.

"Dang it, Ford, why did you take notes for me? Why did you rush to bring them to me when you could have brought them later? Why are you here?" she shouted and with each punctuated word my own irritation at her prodding grew.

"Because I was fucking worried that something had happened to you, okay? Is that what you wanted to hear?" I roared, my entire body opening up as I unleashed on her. "You weren't answering texts and you never miss class, even when you have a cold you sit in that damned seat annoying the shit out of me with your sniffles. So, excuse me if I felt an ounce of concern for you. But don't worry, it won't happen again."

I wasn't sure who moved first, but our bodies collided against each other and our lips met in a feverish crash. My hands sought out the soft skin around her waist, slipping through the opening in her sheet that was knotted above her breasts. Her body shook as I trailed my fingers around her waist and toward her ass.

"Ford," she whispered as she nipped at my bottom lip. "Bedroom, now."

By command, I bent slightly and slid an arm along the backside of her knees, lifting her in the air. As we traveled down the hall, Jolee pressed her mouth against the side of my neck and I nearly collapsed against the wall as she nibbled at the skin. Fuck, how had she seemed to find the one spot that could bring me to my knees? That one patch of skin just below my earlobe - a single nibble and I was a goner.

Gently I laid us on the bed, her sheet still firmly wrapped around her, but that wasn't going to last long. I stepped over to her bedroom door, closed and locked it. I wasn't sure if her roommates were around, but we didn't need an audience for what I planned to do.

My leather jacket fell on the floor with a plop and my shirt quickly joined it. I walked toward the bed watching Jolee's large brown eyes dilate with need.

"It's really not fair how hot you are."

Grabbing her ankles, I pulled her legs apart, the sheet masking the sweet center I was after.

"No, what's really not fair is this damn sheet blocking my view."

In a flash, I yanked the ends of the damn piece of cotton and opened it like the best kind of birthday present. And I was definitely thrilled with what I found lying underneath.

"Ford," she begged as I leaned toward her ankle and pressed my lips against the skin. I was determined to take my time as I worked my way up the inside of one leg, then the other. Jolee was writhing against my hands that gripped at her thighs. Her scent was floating around me as I reached the apex of her thighs and my mouth watered at her delectable flavor.

"Ford, no one has. . ." she trailed off as she spoke. I knew she was no virgin, but how could a man hold himself back from tasting her? It nearly killed me last time.

"Well, they were idiots."

Her answering chuckle lingered in the room but disappeared as she gasped when I pressed a kiss against her slit. My tongue joined and followed the wet path up toward her pleasure button hidden beneath a rose-colored hood.

I swirled my tongue around her clit, loving how she jerked her hips silently requesting more. My finger slid inside her effortlessly as I continued to lick and suck her clit into my mouth. I used her wetness to glide my fingers up and down her folds coating her body in her own honey.

"Ford, I'm going to come," she said as she sunk her hand into my hair, gripping the ends as she rocked against my mouth.

Jolee's body arched off the bed as she climaxed and I watched captivated by her.

As she slowly came back into herself, Jolee murmured, "Oh my gosh." While her eyes were trained on mine, I slipped the two fingers that had been deep inside her sex into my mouth. I could get addicted to her flavor, the perfect mix of sweetness and something uniquely Jolee.

With closed eyes, I stood up and tried to pinpoint exactly what she tasted like when I felt her fingertips on my belt. My cock was straining against my jeans, begging to escape, and now it begged for her touch.

"You don't have to," I told her as I placed my hand gently on her wrist and looked down, but damn, just seeing her crouched on the bed in front of me with eager eyes about did me in.

"I want to." Then Jolee did something that would haunt my best dreams – she licked those beautiful lips of hers in anticipation. It was such an innocent move but filled my mind with the naughtiest of possibilities.

While I had been busy fantasizing about her mouth on my cock, she had guided the zipper down and was gathering the edges of my pants and boxer briefs to jerk them down. A ringing sound filled the room and Jolee looked up at me in confusion until I realized that it was the phone in my back pocket.

"Sorry," I said as she reached around my ass and grabbed the device. Her eyes flickered down at the screen for a second then she looked back up at me. A crease had grown between her brows as she held the phone up, the name *Heather* lit up on the screen. If a ringing phone alone didn't squelch the mood, a woman's name certainly would.

The ringing stopped before I could answer and all thoughts about Jolee's lips around my cock disappeared. The facility's director didn't call for no reason. We had scheduled times in the evening for those.

Jolee had already moved back onto the bed as I placed my phone back into my pocket and reclosed my pants.

"I have to go," I told her as I turned around and gathered my shirt, tugging it over my head.

"Oh, of course you do. Don't let me keep you." I could hear the anger and hurt in her voice. Only my brothers knew of the situation with my mother and I didn't have enough time to explain it to Jolee. I still wasn't sure if I even wanted to.

I didn't bother putting on my jacket knowing that I was heading back to campus and I needed the cold air to help take care of the erection throbbing in my jeans.

"Thanks for the notes," she sarcastically added as she went over to her dresser and started roughly tossing clothes onto her bed.

I wanted to call out her name, wanted to put her mind at ease that I wasn't leaving for another woman, at least not in the way she assumed. But I didn't have the time, nor did I think that she would listen.

"It's not what you think," I told her as I made my way down her hall to leave.

"If you think I'm upset, think again. At least I got off."

God, this woman. Sometimes I really wanted to strangle her.

I didn't reply as I slammed her apartment door closed and made my way downstairs, dialing Heather's number as I went.

"Heather," I said as she answered my call.

"Thank you for calling me back so quickly, Ford."

"Did something happen with my mother?" My fears had grown to insurmountable levels by the time I reached my own room. I ignored my brothers as I shut my door and leaned my back against the wooden surface.

"Your mother is doing fine. She's helping to prepare some of the residents for the afternoon activity."

"Then why the abrupt call in the middle of the day?" Not to mention the interruption during my time with Jolee.

"Well, it seems that early this morning there was an unexpected visitor requesting information on your mother," she relayed as I breathed a sigh of relief knowing that my mother was doing well. I had received calls like this before, usually due to an accident where she stayed. I knew Brent was going to try and look up my mother's health records. It seemed plausible that he may go to her facility. Just as I was about to chime in with that information, Heather said something that changed everything. "And, Ford, they were asking about you, too."

"Me?" I questioned. I was in a daze as I slid down the door until my backside hit the floor.

"The security guard was given five thousand dollars to give up any information he had on you and your mother. Thankfully, he came straight to me instead.

"I've known you and your mother for a long time now. You're like family. I don't know what's going on but stay safe, Ford. We'll look out for your mother."

"Will you let me know if he comes back or if anyone else starts snooping around?"

"Of course."

"Thank you, Heather."

"Take care, Ford."

My head banged against the door as I replayed in my mind what she had just informed me. Someone was asking about me and I knew without a doubt that it was my sperm donor or one of his henchmen.

Somehow Senator Hastings found out that I was digging up dirt on him and I had no doubts that he was going to do all he could to stop me.

Glancing down at my mobile, I pressed the number to call Brent and inform him of what was happening. He assured me that he'd keep his eyes peeled and hurry to close up his investigation before my father got to him. I already knew that my father could ruin someone's life; I didn't need to give him more ammunition.

I needed to stay focused and get this all wrapped up. There was no time to wallow in self-pity, my father had been pulling strings behind the scenes ever since I was forced into adoption.

Crawling off the floor I went to my desk and began sifting through the materials I had already gathered. Brent and I were so close I could taste it.

A knock on my door sounded and Link's voice rang out, "Ford, you okay?"

"Yeah, just had a call about my mom," I explained, trying to defend my rush through the apartment as I shoved the paperwork back into the manila envelope.

"Ok, well, we're heading on campus to get lunch with Tracy. Want to come?"

I did want to come, but not in the way he thought. I wanted to finish what Jolee and I had started, but if ever there was a time to back off, it seemed like now would be that moment. Except I tended to lose my head when she was around.

"You know what? Lunch sounds good. I'll be right out."

The only way I knew to distract myself from my father and Jolee was to join the family that would probably hate me if they knew what I had been doing.

I followed Jolee from the apartment complex as she headed toward the business building for our economics midterm. I stayed far enough away that she didn't see me, but I was close enough that I could see her shiver beneath her puffy jacket.   I'm pretty certain Link told me that she was from Alaska, shouldn't she be used to the cold? Either way, I was transfixed by the way she wrapped her arms around her body. It was bitterly cold outside and even I shook beneath my leather jacket. A storm had been brewing and threatened to drop rain and early seasonal snow. The gray clouds lingered above us as we took the steps into the building. I continued to trail behind Jolee as she took the flight of stairs up to the third floor.

My desire to claim her seat was ever present, but even the jerk that I was didn't want to mess with her head the day of midterms. So instead, when she smugly claimed her seat, that cocky grin of hers showcasing a perfect smile, I took the seat next to her.

"Ford," she growled. I knew she didn't want me anywhere near her since our tryst on Monday, but she was going to have to put up with me for one more day. Teasing and irritating her brought me the most enjoyment I had ever had. And I knew that she felt the same.

Her two friends took their seats and I watched as the rest of the class filled in the spots on the other half of the room, watching me with curious eyes. They took Monday's seating arrangement as a one-off, it was no secret around campus that Jolee and I didn't get along. Now the other students were filled with questions. I couldn't imagine what the student body would think if they knew the only time Jolee and I got along was when we were between the sheets.

The professor walked in and did his usual tug of the door to make sure that it was locked. He reached into his bag and grabbed the exams and answer sheets. Jolee had been fidgeting with her phone on her desk, preparing to put it in her bag, but I glanced over and saw that her hand was shaking as she read a text message. From my seat, all I could read was the name Ken and a picture of a dog.

As the teacher approached our row, Jolee hastily placed her phone in her bag and wiped her cheek, but not before I witnessed a tear spill over her lower lid. I may hate her most of the time, but I didn't want to see her cry.

I wasn't sure how she managed to finish her exam; I could barely focus with her sitting next to me. I had just completed the test when Jolee stood up to turn in her answer sheet.

"I'll take it," I whispered as I reached for her paper and she handed it to me without a word. The professor nodded as I sat the papers on his desk and I waited at the door for Jolee to finish grabbing her things.

Together we exited the room, but she was completely distracted, texting on her phone and choking back a sob. I heard the hitch in her breathing, and if we weren't walking in a hallway with other students milling about, I would have grabbed her and wrapped her in my arms. Even if only for her comfort and not my selfish ways.

Her fingers flew across the screen of her phone, her eyes locked on whatever conversation she was having with Ken – the notion that a man was causing her tears wasn't sitting well with me. She was so distracted as we entered the stairwell that she almost missed the first step. On instinct, I reached out and gathered her bicep in my hand.

"Oh," she shrieked as if I'd brought her back into the moment.

"Jolee, are you okay?"

"I. . . I need to go." Tugging her arm, she escaped my grip and began a fast-paced descent down the stairs. I eagerly followed.

"Wait up, Jolee," I bellowed as we reached the first floor, drawing the attention of the people in the café.

"No, I need to go. The shelter needs me, not that I'd expect you to understand that."

The shelter? That was about three blocks from the campus. And as I glanced out the glass doors, I noticed that there was the equivalent of a monsoon outside.

"Let me take you."

"Right. Why would you do that?" she sneered, her small foot tapping against the tiled floor.

"I don't know. But I can get Link to bring my car. I'd feel better knowing that you're not walking around in this mess."

I focused on her elegant neck as she peered over her shoulder toward the doors. As she turned back to me, I could see that she realized how terrible the weather had become.

"Against all of my better judgment, I am going to accept your help. But I need to get there quickly. There isn't much time."

Blindly reaching for my phone in my pocket, I pressed the number for Link and he answered immediately. I asked him to drive my car to the parking lot at the back of the business building and he agreed without question.

"He'll be here soon," I said, but Jolee's attention was back on her phone, her fingers flying across the screen as she typed.

It wasn't but five minutes later that Link sent me a message that he was in the parking lot.

"Come on, Jolee. He's here." She startled as I placed my hand at her lower back.

"Oh, okay. We need to hurry."

Our bodies were soaked as we ate up the short distance from the building to the car. The rain had seeped through our jackets, shirts, and pants down to our skin. Luckily the heat in the car had just kicked in when I slipped into the driver's seat, Link being smart enough to bring an umbrella with him. He didn't even raise a questioning eye to me as Jolee took her spot on the passenger seat, the gentle shake of his head was all I needed to see.

I slammed the door shut and glanced over to my partner, her body shaking off the cold against my leather seat. The water would ruin the seats, but I didn't care.

"Ready?" I asked her as I pulled the car out of the lot, glancing in the rearview mirror to find a black town car behind me. I squinted as I tried to figure out who was driving the vehicle, but I was interrupted when Jolee shockingly said, "Your car is sexy."

"Thanks, I think."

Running her hand along the dashboard, she took her time admiring the vinyl. "It's very you," she added.

"Adam and I rebuilt this car when I was in high school."

She turned those curious eyes toward me and anxiously waited for me to tell her more as we stopped at the stoplight.

"Adam was my adoptive father. He died a few years ago." My eyes were trained on the road as the light turned green. I also wasn't sure if I could look at her and witness that pitiful stare most people gave when they found out about my adoptive father. She touched me gently with her hand on my forearm.

"I'm so sorry for your loss, Ford. I don't know what that must have been like for you."

"It's fine. I'm over it," I lied as I pulled into the animal shelter's parking lot.

"Ford. . ." The way she said my name felt like the lightest of kisses against my ear. I turned my gaze to Jolee's and I was shocked to find compassion in her eyes – not pity. It made me wonder if maybe she did have an understanding of what it felt like to lose someone close to you.

Jolee began to pull her hand away from my arm, and just from the short period we were together in the car, I wasn't ready for my time with her to be up yet.

"Thank you for the-"

"Can I come in with you?" I interrupted.

Jolee blinked up at me in disbelief.

Just for good measure, I added, "Please."

I could see that she fought an inner battle with herself as she weighed my words, her eyes flicking back and forth between mine.

"Okay," she murmured, looking stunned at herself for agreeing.

I turned off the car and shoved my keys in my pocket before gripping the door and making my escape. I dashed behind Jolee in the rain and we skirted to a stop just inside a back entrance to the building.

"Let me take you to the locker room so we can put your jacket away. Ken may have a change of clothes when you're ready to leave." Her hands twisted in front of her body in a nervous gesture and then she bit her bottom lip. If we had been anywhere else, I would have found a place to tuck us away from prying eyes and sucked that lip into my mouth.

I was knocked free from my inner thoughts as a good-looking guy turned the corner and frowned when he saw me standing with Jolee.

"Ken, this is Ford. He drove me."

The man looked me up and down and turned his attention back to Jolee. I knew that he found me lacking when it came to the woman standing beside me and I almost wanted to reach out and wrap my arm around her waist to lay my claim. But knowing Jolee, she'd probably glare at me and figure out a way to torment me later.

"Rocky came in. He isn't doing well; his heart is giving out. I know how close you were with him."

"I'll go sit with him for a while. Thanks for letting me be here."

"Of course. He's in his usual run."

Jolee guided me to a small locker room where she hung our things, then we walked toward the far end of the facility. Dogs barked loudly around us, but Jolee didn't seem fazed at all while I wished that I had earplugs. We walked through a door that led to tall fenced-in spaces that had small openings to private outside areas. I followed her dutifully as dogs jumped on the doors to get Jolee's attention, but she was focused on a kennel at the end of the path.

"Hey, big guy," she muttered as she opened the gate.

A skinny black Labrador laid on a raised bed of blankets. Gray hair covered his muzzle and I knew without asking that this dog was old, but as I took in the shaved parts of his body, I could tell he had been injured recently. His tail moved up and down flapping against the concrete as Jolee stepped inside.

She crouched down beside him and let him smell her hand before she pet his head. The dog's eyes closed at her touch. "This is Rocky. He was hit by a car a few weeks ago and they brought him in. It's why I stayed late that one night. . ."

"The night I made a fool out of myself."

Finally, a smirk grew on her lips as she settled on the floor beside Rocky's head. "I don't know. I had a pretty good time that night."

"Can I pet him?" I asked, not sure of the protocol.

"Sure, just let him sniff your hand first. Rocky's usually tame, but you never know."

I held my hand a foot in front of him, but Jolee grabbed my fingers and pulled them all the way up to the dog's muzzle. Glancing at Jolee in exasperation, I left my hand lingering for a moment against Rocky's wet nose. His tail flicked up and down a few times and I smiled at

Jolee in excitement. Gently I reached forward and ran my hand across the top of his head. I had always loved animals but knew that having a pet was out of the question, Tracy and Adam worked too much to take care of a pet plus all of us boys.

Jolee kicked her legs out as she got comfortable against the wall and I settled on the floor with my legs crossed.

Filling the silence, I looked over to Jolee who had closed her eyes and rested her head against the wall. She looked beautiful. "You know, I've never been in an animal shelter before," I confessed.

"Really?"

I shrugged my shoulders.

"This is my dream," she whispered, opening her eyes to meet mine. Something different was passing between us for a second, I forgot that we were sitting in the middle of a dingy kennel. Everything else around us faded away – the sound of dog barks echoing in the room, the smell of animals, the knowledge of my past. It was just Jolee and me, and I did something I had never done before.

"Tell me about it."

RENEE HARLESS

CHAPTER ELEVEN

JOLEE

To say I was shocked when Ford asked me about my dream was an understatement. At first, I thought that I had heard him wrong, but after I asked him to clarify what he meant, he asked me to tell him why I said that was my dream.

"I want to open an animal rescue. I volunteered at a local Alaskan rescue and I knew that was what I wanted to do with my life."

"Wow, I'm shocked."

"Why?" I questioned. Leave it to this gorgeous man gently petting Rocky to assume that I couldn't run a rescue.

"No, no. I've just. . .never felt so inadequate before. I see you, this stunningly beautiful girl that has this amazing goal for her life. While most people have zero ideas what they'll do when they graduate – myself included."

I could feel my cheeks flame at his compliment. Ford and I had warmed his bed before, but he'd never outright complimented my looks, and frankly, it felt nice.

"I'm sure you have an idea of what you'd like to do. I don't even know your major."

It was the first time I had seen Ford look embarrassed as he tucked his chin closer to his chest. "Dual. I'm getting a degree in both mathematics and astronomy."

My jaw hung open at his declaration. "Wow, talk about feeling inadequate. I knew you were smart, but geez. If only the women on campus knew that the good looks also came with a brain," I tried to joke and he answered with a soft chuckle. "So, you have no idea what you can do with those degrees?"

"No. I mean, I have some ideas, but I just thought I'd see what happens after graduation this year. Aerospace, analytics, astrophysics, maybe go on for my masters. I don't know yet."

I blinked in awe of him. Did he have any idea how incredible he sounded describing his career choices? Watching him speak, it seemed as if he was used to being criticized, as if he was ashamed. I was so beyond impressed there were no words.

"And to think I had a genius kicking my chair this semester. Why are you in my class anyway?"

"I'm only in the economics course to fill a general education credit. Why are you in there? What's your major?"

Together we killed time helping Rocky relax by making small talk. I told him about my degree in Biology and how I transferred here to be closer to my cousin, Willow, and I was fulfilling the master's prerequisites. At some point, Rocky had fallen asleep, the short sporadic bursts of air from his lungs concerned me, but there wasn't much I could do but continue to pet him as he slept. I knew that it brought him comfort. At some point, Ford, in his now dingy black jeans, moved beside me.

"So, tell me more about the shelter," he said.

"I just. . . love animals and wildlife. I want to help rescue and heal them, take care of them if they're orphaned, protect them if they're unable to return to the wild." Maybe that was what connected me with Ford - he was just like the animals I yearned to care for.

"Will you move home to open it?"

I tossed around how to answer the question. Should I give him the short version of wanting to spread my wings? Or should I go all in and explain why I left home to begin with? Ford wasn't the kind of guy to stick around for the long term, so I didn't have anything to lose by laying it all out there. I feared that the revelation would bring us closer. I just had to remember that Ford wasn't boyfriend material, nor did I want one.

"I'm not sure I'll return to Alaska. I have to go home during winter break, but after that?" I shrugged my shoulders as if that completed my statement.

"I'm guessing there is more to the story, isn't there?"

"How about this? If I tell you mine, you tell me yours. It's only fair."

He smirked at me, and with his face so close, it took all my inner strength to keep from leaning forward and kissing him senseless.

"We both know that I never play fair." That was the definite truth.

"What do you have to lose? It's just Rocky and me." The dog beneath my palm perked up at the sound of his name but immediately fell back to sleep.

"Okay. You start."

"Fine. As I just told you, I'm from Alaska, a small town just outside of Anchorage. It's beautiful there.

"It wasn't until I started middle school that I realized how strange my parents were. I mean, I knew that they were sort of odd, but they spent every weekend traveling around the city researching aliens – specifically the Japan Airlines Flight 1628. It's pretty famous for crashing due to an alien encounter.

"As a young kid, I thought it was completely normal, but you know how cruel kids can be, right? I learned early on that my parents were different, so I kept quiet about all of the plane crashes and recordings they investigated with friends. They call themselves researchers, but they're no different than ambulance chasers that somehow secure grants for funding. Neither of my parents has actual jobs."

I had turned my attention to Rocky as I spoke, but I was surprised when I turned my head to glance at Ford. He had bent one knee and rested his elbow on top, using his hand to support his chin. He looked as if he was genuinely interested in what I was saying. I couldn't fight against the small smile that grew on my lips.

"Is that why you came to Boston? To get away from your parents' strange lifestyle?"

I shook my head before responding. "No. Heck, I wish my parents being weird was the worst thing I had to go through. I left because I needed to escape."

Ford tensed at my words, and I wish that I had described it better, but it was exactly what I had done against my parents' wishes – I escaped to save myself. I immediately moved my attention back to Rocky. This was the part that changed how people saw me. It changed how I saw myself.

"In high school, I began dating the new boy in school. The people that were my so-called friends began to despise me for it. But I was blissfully unaware, you know?" I took a heavy and deep breath that filled my lungs as I reached the next part of my story – the story that defined who I was today. "At a summer party, David, my boyfriend, and I were kissing under a shaded willow tree while his friends hung around the bonfire. There was music, drinking, and everyone was being loud and raucous, you know? We were all sixteen and excited for the summer.

"David. . .he, um. . .spiked my drink and took my virginity from me without my consent. The drink had pretty much paralyzed my body but I had my wits about me. It was agonizing, I felt the pain, I felt. . .everything. And what made it worse was that his friends knew what he was doing. One even got a grainy video on his phone.

"I went to the police and had a test, but. . .you see, David's father was the new head of the police department and pulled strings to have everything ignored. Even though there was a video, everyone said I had asked for it. The ridicule and teasing became too much. There was no way I was returning to school. My mother ended up homeschooling me until I graduated.

"My parents did a complete one-eighty after the incident. They went from free-spirited hippies to strict and orthodox. The constant overbearing nature became too much, so once I fulfilled my biology degree, I took Willow up on the offer to move here.

"So, that's it, that's my story," I declared as I returned my gaze to his.

Before I could utter another word, Ford reached a hand up to the back of my head and drew me in for a kiss. It was unlike anything I had ever experienced. We had been both passionate and unyielding in our desires before, but this kiss spoke of so much more. Strength. Comprehension. Need. Ford's lips were pressed against mine as if he couldn't fathom them being anywhere else. He was trying to take my pain into himself. The pain of being an outcast, of being demoralized, of having my childhood stolen. He possessed me with the simplest of kisses. And if I had thought for one second that I had the power to preserve my heart from him, I had been sorely mistaken. It only took a single kiss to realize that I had fallen for him — hook, line, and sinker. I fell for the man that kept himself tucked behind a wall of concrete and I only hoped that I could chisel away at its exterior.

Ford pulled back, just enough so that he could run his hand across my hair, like he was making sure that I was real. "Was I the first after. . .you know?" he asked.

And I swore that I saw disappointment flash across his face when I shook my head. "No, I, uh, had a couple of one-night stands, but never any relationships. I've steered clear of them, to be honest."

I couldn't tell if he was relieved or saddened by the realization that I had been with others since the incident.

"I'm okay, Ford. I've just spent a lot of time focusing on school and what it will take to get my animal rescue off the ground. Relationships haven't been particularly important. I saw a therapist for a while and I've learned that none of it was my fault.

"David may have been cleared of all charges, but karma came back around. He was in a bad car accident his freshman year of college and lost his football scholarship because he had been drunk. I'm fairly certain he is working at the fish market now."

"You're pretty incredible, you know that?"

"So, what's your story? What makes Ford, Ford?"

I could see that he was weighing his answer deliberately, deciding what ugly parts to keep secret. I had hoped that by telling him the deepest and most dreadful part of me that he would be willing to do the same. But Ford reminded me so much of the animals I yearned to care for. He was skittish and would always protect himself first.

"Rutherford. My full name is Rutherford James O'Brien and my birth father is Senator Rutherford Hastings."

Ford quieted the instant the words left his mouth and I wondered if he wished he could take them back. I didn't know much about politics, but Senator Hastings was very well known and rumors swirled that he was gearing for a presidential run. But my memory of Senator Hastings was of a much older man with a trophy wife at his side. I knew his children were closer to my parents' age, so imagining him as Ford's father was proving to be extremely difficult. There was a resemblance, though. Something that I immediately recognized when Ford turned to me – his eyes. The sparkling blue irises and long lashes were identical to his father's. No one would be able to question it. But at the same time, it left me wondering how his mother was involved.

Senator Hastings was known as a family man. Tabloids and papers published pictures of him with his children and grandchildren. I was pretty confident I had seen some reports on television. I wasn't well versed, but no one had ever mentioned affairs or illegitimacy.

"My mother worked for Hastings as an assistant while she was working through law school. She was young and naive, and he took advantage of that. My mother never gave me the sordid details, but when she fell pregnant, he had made promises that he had zero intentions of keeping. He wanted my mother to abort me, but she wouldn't.

"He was furious and made all kinds of threats to her and her family. But all she asked was that he sign my birth certificate in his name as my father and she would never come after a single penny. She's kept her word all these years."

My mind was drowning as I tried to keep up with the information. It all seemed like something from a movie – not real life. How could people be so cruel and deliberately take advantage of someone?

"I'm trying to grasp everything you're telling me. What happened to your mother? I thought you were adopted."

Ford's eyes glazed over as I asked my question. His entire body tensed and then quickly dissolved as he brought his knees toward his chest, rested his arms on top, then drooped his head over the crossed limbs.

"I've never told anyone what happened, Jolee. My cousin suspects, but it's never been out in the open."

"You don't have to tell me, Ford. It's okay." And it was. He had shared more than I ever imagined, and while we were here in the dirty dog kennel, it seemed as if our confessions had brought us closer together.

"No, no. I need to tell someone. I'm pretty certain it's been eating away at me for so long that I'm hollow inside."

Ford's back rose and fell as he took each solid breath, working through whatever secrets he kept locked away. I waited patiently, rubbing Rocky's soft fur for so long that when Ford began to speak again, I startled.

"When I was four, a group of officers arrived at the apartment my mom and I were living in. It all happened so fast and the screams that came from my mother still wake me at night sometimes.

"I remember the night so vividly. She had been working at a bookstore to pay for school since she could no longer be near the law office where my birth father worked. It was her last year of law school and our neighbor had been watching me whenever mom was gone. She was making my favorite mac and cheese when the officers entered the apartment.

"A social worker immediately scooped me up and placed me in an ugly burgundy car that smelled like burnt popcorn. I screamed out for my mother as they wheeled her out strapped to a gurney.

"I was too young to remember much more than hopping from foster home to foster home until Tracy and Adam took me in. She was the first one to take me to visit my mother in the psychiatric hospital. My mom wasn't crazy, though. I knew it, Tracy knew it, and so did the caregivers, but they were forced by the state to keep her confined in the building.

"I think after so long, my mother gave up trying to fight it. Every appeal and case she tried to take to the courts was thrown out. Every single one for almost twenty years."

This tale he wove seemed so outrageous that I couldn't wrap my head around all of the details. She was living a mother's worst nightmare and there was nothing she could do to stop it. Realization dawned on me suddenly and I had never felt so low in my entire life. "Ford, I can't. . .I can't believe I had said that thing about your mother and how she raised you. No wonder you looked like you could have strangled me if you had the chance," I confessed shamefully. I wanted to dig myself a grave and bury myself in it.

"It's okay. You didn't know."

"It's not okay. Not at all," I argued.

Ford suddenly sat up and ran his hand through his hair as he looked over at me. "It is, just drop it."

"Fine. So, what do you think happened?"

"I think my sperm donor and his family set up my mother."

Ford said this with such conviction, as if there was no other possible explanation and no one would be able to convince him otherwise. I wanted to ask more, I wanted to understand if this was why he was so closed off from everyone, but beneath my hand, I noticed that Rocky's shallow breathing had halted.

"Oh, no," I whimpered as I turned away from Ford and pressed my other hand to the Labrador's chest.

"What happened?" Ford asked as he crawled along the floor to get a better look at the dog.

"He was tired and gave up the fight." Forcing a smile on my lips I glanced at Ford, who had shifted again onto his backside. He glared at me as if I had ended Rocky's life myself.

"Gave up? How could he give up? He has a family that loves him and needs him to fight for his life. Didn't he know that?"

It donned on me that Ford and Rocky were synonymous. Each of them had something significant and life-changing happen to them. Rocky's fate had been determined, but Ford's was still up in the air.

Despite my sadness at Rocky's passing, the dog essentially was the reason Ford and I had come together to begin with. I spun toward Ford and laid my hand on his wrist to get his attention.

"He was ready to go, Ford. Rocky was comfortable with us here, probably happy, to be honest. Sometimes we have to learn to let go."

From beside me, Ford's body shook slightly, and I couldn't help but call out his name again to get his attention. "Ford."

I'm not sure what I had been expecting when he would respond, but seeing the tears building across his eyes, the blue swirling like a whirlpool, drew me closer.

"Come on. I'll let Ken know about Rocky, but there is another place I want to show you. It's my favorite place to go when something like this happens."

We said our goodbyes to Rocky and I was comforted knowing that when the sweet Labrador passed, he felt love and kindness from Ford and me. Ken seemed to be equally as heartbroken when I told him the news, but my friend was much quicker at composing himself.

As I guided Ford down another hall, I reached out a comforting hand toward him, and I was surprised at how he latched onto it. His rough fingers interlaced between mine and squeezed. I had never had my hand held like this, as if I were his lifeline. My mind raced from thoughts of me and Ford, a great distraction from what had happened with Rocky, that I almost missed the door to what I liked to call Happiness Hallway. All of the other staff referred to it as Mess Hall.

"Here we are!" I exclaimed as I turned to look at Ford, hoping he could channel some of the excitement I was feeling.

"Where is here?"

With an enthusiastic smile, I pulled my hand from Ford's and used it to slide my badge through the electronic lock and open the door.

Loud and overzealous barking ensued as the door opened farther into the space.

"This is where we keep all of the puppies. If you prefer kittens, they are across the way, but I always find that puppies are much better attuned to my sadness, personally."

It took a moment of Ford walking in the space and witnessing the overenthusiastic pups as they bounced and squirmed in their kennels wanting his attention for his frown to dissipate. I opened the gate to the first kennel and stepped inside, immediately closing the door to the escape artists, where about five mixed-breed puppies jumped on their hind legs for us. I scooped one up in my arms and set him in Ford's. The puppy blinked at Ford and then licked at his chin. We both laughed at the puppy's excited kisses.

"Yeah, this isn't so bad," Ford said as I sat with my back against the gate and allowed the remaining puppies to crawl all over me. "I can see why you want to open a shelter."

"Rescue," I clarified. "We will be able to shelter animals if they are unable to return to the wild, but I want to save and return the ones that I can. We can't stop the circle of life, you know, but I want to do whatever I can to help the helpless."

Once the puppies in the kennel had had their fill, zonking out in the corner, we moved through the remaining five runs. Puppies would get very jealous if they didn't get equal attention.

"You said you studied Biology, right?"

"Yep," I said, holding a Border Collie puppy that was missing one eye. The breeder didn't want to keep a dog that he couldn't sell. I kind of wanted to keep the puppy for myself. "I have a degree in Biology with a concentration in wildlife and conservation."

"Wow, ever think of being a veterinarian?"

"I did, for a long time, but the veterinarian field is very specialized when you plan on opening a business. Like, I'd have to decide on large animals, reptiles, that sort of thing. With a rescue, I can help so much more."

I let the Border Collie puppy back on the ground and turned to glance at Ford, who was gazing at me with a look of awe and amazement. I blushed under his watchful eye, and as I stood up, I flustered opening the gate.

He followed behind me and we ran into Ken near the locker room. I thanked him for calling me so that I could be with Rocky.

Ford and I didn't have a change of clothes, so we both appeared to have been rolling in dog hair, but neither of us seemed to mind. He even chuckled as he pulled his shirt away from his body and shook it out, mounds of dog hair floating to the floor. Reaching into the locker for my bag and Ford's jacket, I almost ate my own tongue when I turned to find Ford pulling his shirt over his head.

"What are you doing?" I asked, glancing around like someone would actually yell at him for showing his incredible chest and abs. I found myself wishing that I could lick at that darn V that ran across the front of his hips and slithered beneath his jeans.

"I have a shirt in my car I can put on," he explained as he reached for his jacket.

"Yeah, but it's freezing outside. You'll get sick."

He laughed in a way that crept across my skin like a snake, wrapping itself around me until I could do nothing more than succumb to its power. "That's what I have a jacket for. Now, take yours off. I have a shirt you can wear."

Hypnotized by his spell, I found myself tugging my sweater over my head without a second thought. Ford helped slip my jacket over my body and zipping, the still damp material went all the way up to my chin.

"Let's go."

Our hands intertwined as we made a mad dash from the building to his car in the pouring rain. Ford even stood in the downpour, holding my door open until I was settled inside, before moving toward his own.

"Oh my gosh, will this rain ever stop?"

"Eh, it's supposed to be like this through the weekend."

"That stinks. But I guess it's a good thing I'll be staying inside."

Ford started the engine for the car and pulled it out of the parking lot. "No plans for Thanksgiving?" he asked as we turned onto the street.

"No. Just going to hang out at the apartment. You?"

"Tracy has us all over and her family from Carson, North Carolina comes in to town. It's a big thing."

"That must be nice."

Silence filled the car as Ford refrained from saying anything else. I wondered if he imagined having a large feast with his mother or if he had ventured back to the incidents regarding his father.

"I want to do something for you since you allowed me to kidnap you and trail along today pretty much," Ford said nervously. His voice was shallow and tight as he spoke, something I had never heard from him before. And as I turned in my seat to take him in, he was gripping the steering wheel, twisting his hands back and forth along the leather.

"You don't have to do anything, Ford. But what did you have in mind?"

"I want to take you to dinner."

Shock and disbelief ran through me because I knew from Willow and Haley that they had never known any of the ridge rouges to do more than go to bed with a woman. Dates were not part of their repertoire.

I murmured, "Like a date," barely able to get the words out.

"Yeah."

He seemed so uncomfortable, that despite my excitement, I gave him an out. "It's okay, Ford. You don't have to do anything for me. It was nice to have you there today."

His head turned toward me quickly and one wet clump of his hair draped over his eye. "I want to. . .with you."

"Okay," I complied, and needing to break the tension that I had caused, I added, "But I'm going to need that shirt. Otherwise, the restaurant is going to get an eyeful."

His laughter joined my giggle and thankfully the remainder of the car ride was filled with Ford asking me more questions about opening a rescue. I was amazed at how interested he seemed in the work I wanted to do.

Ford pulled into the same pub where Willow, Haley, and I had seen him and his family. He handed me a shirt from the backseat. At first, I was worried that it would smell like sweat or musty, but it didn't. It smelled like being wrapped in a Ford blanket.

"You're not getting this back, you know," I said as I slipped the Metallica shirt over my head and smirked at him as he did the same with another shirt.

Together we dashed into the pub, which wasn't very full. It was that time between lunch and dinner, but since Ford and I had skipped the previous meal, we were starving. The same server as before took our order, both of us opting for soup and sandwiches instead of something more substantial.

Ford's phone sat on the table, and throughout the meal, he continued to glance at the screen. I wasn't annoyed, but more or less concerned. After learning everything about his mother and father, I would imagine that someone would constantly have to be on the lookout. Because if Senator Hastings was trying to hide Ford, I couldn't imagine the lengths that he would go to.

I choked on a piece of bread at the notion of Ford's father trying to rid himself of his son completely. It took a forceful gulp of water to get the rest of the sandwich down.

"You okay?" Ford asked as I coughed a few times, trying to get air back into my lungs.

"Yeah, sorry. It went down the wrong pipe," I lied. I was afraid of how Ford would react if I told him my thoughts and theories about his father. My heart lurched thinking about how wrong I could be – of how wrong Ford could be in his assumptions. "Are you okay?" I changed the subject and gestured to his phone.

"Yeah, sorry. I'm just waiting for a call and I was going to go see my mother when we're done."

"Oh my gosh, don't let me keep you. Is she close by?"

"Yeah, she lives about forty minutes away."

Gripping the sandwich in my hand, I took the last two bites until my cheeks were puffed out like a chipmunk and smiled at Ford, gleefully showing him that I was finished with my meal. He rolled his eyes but flagged down the server to pay.

We remained quiet through the car ride back to the apartment complex, where Ford pulled up to the curb closest to the building. There was a large group of students milling about, so without a backward glance, I opened the door to his car and grabbed my bag. With my hand resting on the top of the door prepared to shut the metal mass, Ford's voice rang out.

"Hey, Jolee," he called and I glanced over my shoulder to find Ford leaning across the seat toward me. "Thanks."

I wanted to ask for what, but instead, I found myself smiling and saying, "You're welcome."

Closing the door, I stepped onto the curb and watched as Ford drove away. I was getting confused at my response to him. There was no denying that we had an attraction, a finite chemistry that attracted us to each other. But there was also the notion that Ford didn't fit into my plans and I didn't fit into his. We could let this unnamed thing between us fizzle out naturally and then go about our days, except nature already fooled us in thinking it was a one-time thing.

Ford's car disappeared down the road as water pooled around me. I turned just in time to bump into a tall and angry man. Through the rain, I could barely make out the man's features. A shiver traveled down my body, not from the cold, but from his icy gaze locked onto mine. I recognized him at that moment, even with his formal dress coat collar pulled up toward his ears.

"Miss Ward, I think you and I have some things to discuss."

My head twisted left and right to see if any of the other students were taking in our encounter, but everyone was too busy dodging the rainstorm.

Harshly I responded, "I have nothing to discuss with you."

"Oh, I'm sure that we do and you're going to listen carefully." The man leaned close to me, more than I felt was necessary. And as his breath ran across my cheek, I had to fight back the urge to gag. I wanted to push him away. I wanted to call him out in front of everyone for the inhumane way he treated Ford and Ford's mother – if what Ford said was true.

"I'm not going to listen to anything," I said, pushing away and cutting toward the apartment complex.

I knew that if Senator Hastings wanted to track me down – he could. It would only be a matter of time. But I wasn't going to let anyone put a damper on my day. I had already dealt with one loss and I wasn't going to be forced into another.

CHAPTER TWELVE

FORD

Visits with my mother were always turbulent. Not because of her or anything she did since my mother was a saint. But seeing her confined in this space, with her fight drained empty, always caused my chest to twist in agonizing pain. Usually, I went home and I lost myself in whatever booze was at the apartment.

"Hey, Mom," I said as I watched her enter a new patient at the nurse's station. She looked so calm and put together in a pressed navy suit and her dark hair pulled in a knot at the back of her head. I imagined that this was how she would look if she had been able to represent clients in the courtroom.

My mother peered up from the computer and her smile stretched across her face in delight. Her dark eyes twinkled in joy and I hoped that one day they'd stay like that permanently.

"Hey, sweetheart," she exclaimed as she dashed around the workspace.

When I learned to drive, I started to visit her more, but with school I could only manage once a week. She didn't seem to mind, though. Meredith had probably worried that she would never see me again after that fateful night. She and Tracy had remained good friends after that first time my foster mother brought me to the facility.

"Sorry that I'm late," I told her as I wrapped her thin frame in my arms. She smiled, always seeming so content with whatever life had thrown her way. I liked to think that I carried the burden around for both of us.

"I'm always happy to see you at whatever hour." And she meant it. My mother was never sad or morose when I appeared, even if it was for a few minutes. Regardless of what life had thrown her way, mostly caused by my despicable sperm donor, Meredith never let on how unhappy she was. She had to be, though. I couldn't imagine having a positive outlook if my life had turned out like hers – my career and son both taken from me without an explanation and no one offering me the chance to make it right.

I hoped that soon my mother would get her justice.

Meredith perked up as she pulled away and she made that same look Tracy made when she thought that I had a secret. "You seem happy today." She wasn't wrong. I was simply waiting on Brent to confirm one more bit of information and I was going to be ecstatic.

"Yeah, my friend took me to an animal shelter and we played with puppies."

"Is this friend a girl?" Shaking my head, I pulled away from my mother and glanced at a few other caregivers sitting at the nurse's station. Everyone was sharing the same knowing smirk and I felt like I was ten standing in front of a group of strangers giving a speech.

"Don't read into it, Mom. She needed a ride."

"You say that, except you make the same face your uncle used to make when he liked a girl. This one is special. I can tell."

I stepped away from her and then took a second and third step back. "Well, Mom, it was great seeing you."

"Oh, come on now. I don't get to tease you enough," she joked and I couldn't fight my answering chuckle.

Screams sounded from down the hall and two nurses rushed around us toward the patient.

"I hate that you're here."

My mom reached out a soothing hand, caressing my face with her thumb. Her touch was soft and gentle, and I found myself tilting my head toward her palm. "You're a good boy."

"If you were free from this place, where is the first place you'd go? What is the first thing that you'd do?"

I'd asked her these questions many times, especially when the ramifications of her living situation became more clearly defined as I got older. The answers always changed, but their center stayed the same. Me – she wanted to be wherever I was. I was always her first thought, as she was mine – except for the time Jolee had been in my bed. That was the only time someone else was my initial thought and it continued to taunt me.

"I want to meet the girl that has you wrapped up in yourself. And I want to watch you stand at the end of a wedding aisle waiting for your bride. And I want to see you happy, Ford. That's all I've ever wanted. I'll stay in this home for the rest of my life so long as you get the chance to live yours."

I felt like I had been on an emotional rollercoaster today and my mom's words took me for another loop. How could she tell Jolee had infiltrated the parts of me I had thought didn't exist? How did she know that there was a girl that made me wish that my life was different, that my situation was different? Nothing would be able to change until I was able to vindicate my mother.

"I don't know anything about marriage. I think you're getting a bit ahead of yourself," I joked and my mother lightly tapped my arm.

"Whatever you say, my boy. But don't forget Tracy and I talk on the phone and I know all about your verbal sparring partner." I was going to wring Tracy's neck and then my brothers' because they had to open their big mouths. "Now, Nathan said he had a nice steak for me for dinner tonight. I'd love it if you sat with me."

Nathan was a world-renowned chef that gave up everything when his youngest sister made multiple attempts at ending her life. When she was admitted to the same facility as my mother, he took it upon himself to become the food provider for the patients. He wanted to make sure that his sister got the best meals and he only knew one way to provide that. Nathan had also taken a liking to my mother. He was only a few years older and my mother was beautiful, looking no older than thirty or so. I also liked Nathan, so I was happy that he kept an eye on my mother as well.

"There is nowhere I'd rather be. Just limit the googly eyes, please."

Dinner was as eventful as I imagined with two middle-aged people making flirtatious comments back and forth at each other. It took everything I had to keep from vomiting all over the table. But I knew that she was delighted to have dinner with both of us. I would just need to bring earplugs next time.

The two of them were in deep discussions about music from the eighties when my phone vibrated in my pocket. Brent's name flashed across the screen and I felt my lungs shrivel up. I had been waiting anxiously all day for his call.

"Hey, Mom. I need to take this. I'll be right outside."

Swiftly I scurried around the tables and made my way outside the dining room doors dialing Brent's number.

"Do you have anything?" I demanded, my words clipped and tight.

At Brent's answering sigh, I immediately deflated against the wall. "The contact was compromised. But they were able to provide me with some information, it's just not enough. I have one more person I'm seeking, then after that. . ." He let his words hang in the air, but I knew what he was referring to. If this person didn't pan out, then there wouldn't be enough evidence to pin anything on my birth father. Years of hard work and hopes for absolution would be for nothing.

It took me a moment to gather myself, to compose what little ounce of hope that remained. One of the nurses walked by and gave me a sympathetic glance.

"When do you think an exchange will take place?" I inquired.

"A week or two. I'm on their timeline."

"Okay. Thanks for the update, Brent."

Ending the call, I knew that I needed to take a moment to settle down. My heart was pounding wildly in my chest.

My problem was that I didn't have a backup plan – everything was riding on Brent gathering this last piece of information. I just knew that it had to exist, but it was proving to be as hard to find as the Loch Ness Monster.

Peering over my shoulder, I look through the glass partition into the dining room where my mother and Nathan were leaned close to each other deep in conversation. My father was robbing her of her life for no other reason than because she had me.

Frustrated, I turned and found the closest wall, pounding my fist into the plaster. Blood oozed from my hand onto the white wall, but I didn't notice the pain, just the shock that there was a chance my mother would spend the rest of her days locked inside this place.

The nurse that had walked by when I took the phone call warily came closer, holding a clean towel for my hand. I thanked her and went back inside to say goodbye to my mother, tucking my injured hand behind my back.

"I love you, Ford."

"I love you too, Mom."

Leaving the facility, I drove my car around aimlessly with no real place in mind. I was lost in my own mind that somehow I ended up at the cemetery where my cousin, Tyler's, parents were buried. I couldn't explain it, but my gut was telling me that my sperm donor was responsible for their deaths as well, but so far, Brent hadn't been able to find anything suggesting that he had been. It just all seemed too fishy for me.

Stepping out of my car, I made my way over to their gravesites, the large marble headstones glistened in the setting sun as the rain dissipated. The cemetery wasn't a place that I often visited, not because it gave me the creeps like it did most people, but because of the guilt that weighed on my shoulders. I couldn't stop thinking that my aunt and uncle would still be alive if my birth father hadn't been a terrible person.

My hand rested on the top of my aunt's headstone. I could remember her laughter and how easy it came. I had wondered for a long time why social services hadn't given me to them, but I quickly realized that the system had been manipulated. Somehow, someway, he had made sure that my entire family, not just me, suffered.

The wind picked up around me, rustling the trees as I let these thoughts loop through my mind.

"I'm sorry that I don't visit more, but I promise you that I'm going to make this right. I'm going to make sure Hastings pays."

The rain that had let off for a few hours opened up and poured through the sky as I stood there talking to pieces of stone. But I didn't feel the cold – my heart was already ice. The only time I felt something different was when I was with Jolee.

I wasn't sure how long I stood out there wallowing in my grief, but the sun had long since set behind the trees painting the sky in blacks and blues.

"I'm sorry, young man, but I'm closing the gate," the guard called out from his vehicle on the path. I was so lost in thought that I didn't hear him approach.

Wordlessly I made my way back to my car and turned out of the cemetery. Even with the heat on high, my body trembled from the wet cold, but there would never be enough warmth to defrost my insides.

Link was sitting in his usual spot on the couch, watching a movie on the television as I walked into the apartment.

"Dude, you're soaking wet. You'll catch pneumonia like that," he exclaimed as he jumped from the couch and rushed toward me. Making quick work, he relieved me of my jacket as I stood like a statue.

"Where have you been?"

"Cemetery. Mom's."

Link stopped halfway to the laundry area and looked back at me, my leather jacket dripping water onto the floor.

"Ford."

The way he said my name hinted at pity and sympathy that I didn't need or want.

"I'm going to go take a shower." I stomped away, leaving wet footprints in my wake, not giving two shits about the water I was leaving on the carpet. In the bathroom, I tugged the soaked clothes off my body, letting them fall onto the vinyl flooring with a plop.

The cold water pierced my skin like razor blades as it heated up, but once it reached its normal temperature, I still felt like ice. It wasn't until thoughts of the blonde living above me soared through my mind that I felt warmth seep through my body.

My hand drifted down to my dick as I remembered the way she let me fuck her even after everything that she had gone through. Her skin was soft and sweet, and there was no doubt that she had the best tasting pussy I had ever put my mouth on. But sinking into her had about done me in. Nothing had ever felt like a fantasy come to life until my cock thrust into her sex.

I was replaying that night with her in my mind, stroking myself in unison until I exploded in my hand. I couldn't remember the last time I had a release but felt no relief from it. My cock wanted Jolee and Jolee only. And that was going to be a major problem because I couldn't have her – not completely, not until everything with Hastings was finished.

By the time I made it out of the shower Link had gone to bed and I wasn't sure if Archer was in his room or out. I gathered my things and went into my own bedroom, tossing the wet clothes in the hamper to wash in the morning.

I glanced at my computer and considered doing more research on my birth father, but I knew that I wasn't going to find anything that I didn't already know. Instead, I reached for a book I hadn't opened in quite some time and did the one thing I knew would take my mind off of everything. I began working on quantum physics word problems.

Link was standing in the entryway, not so patiently waiting for me to get my ass in gear. Tracy was hosting Thanksgiving and we were supposed to be at her house in ten minutes (she lived about twenty-five minutes from the university), but I was dragging. After the visit with my mother yesterday, I wasn't in the right mindset to visit with the makeshift family I was given.

I meandered toward the kitchen, ignoring the way Link was staring at me, except as I opened the fridge and leaned down to look inside I felt my arm jerked backward.

"Hey," I shouted, yanking my arm away from Link's grip.

"Put on a nice shirt and get your ass in gear. You will not disappoint Tracy today. She is expecting all of us."

"Well, I don't feel like going."

"You don't have a choice, Ford, because you know that she'll tell Meredith."

I seethed as he mentioned my mother. He didn't know the level of guilt I was feeling. How could I possibly look at my cousin and try to feel thankful for family? If it wasn't for me, he might still have his.

Suddenly a dark green sweater of Archer's was chucked at my chest. My reflexes were just quick enough to catch it against my body.

My easy-going brother leaned against the counter and said, "Dude, just put it on before Link starts crying."

Our eldest brother turned his narrowed gaze toward Archer as I looked down at the sweater and resigned myself to change. By the time Link and Archer were done silently arguing with each other, I had removed my tattered long-sleeve shirt and replaced it with the sweater.

"Are you ladies done or should I give you two some time alone?"

Both Archer and Link turned their attention to me and I couldn't help but chuckle.

"Asshole," Link murmured as he moved to exit the apartment, Archer and I following behind me.

We made our way to the hallway and I found myself glancing upward as I approached the stairwell. An idea formulated in my mind and I smiled wickedly. If she thought for a moment that she was going to enjoy her Thanksgiving Day by herself, she was mistaken; if I was going to suffer, she was going to suffer too.

"I have to go get somebody," I shouted down to my brothers as I took the stairs to the fourth floor.

BANG. BANG. BANG. My fist beat against her apartment door.

"Hey." Jolee answered with a half-smile on her lips. Part happiness, part confusion.

"You're coming with me," I said as I pushed the door wide and stepped inside just as Archer and Link stepped onto the landing. My Metallica shirt was draped over her body, which secretly thrilled me, but I didn't have time to investigate that emotion.

"I need you to change."

"Excuse me?" she asked, fists planted at her hips as she stopped me from heading toward her bedroom.

"Not like that. I need you to put something nice on. You're coming with me to Tracy's for dinner."

"Why? I was getting ready to start my *Friends* marathon."

"*Friends* can wait. I need you," I explained as I opened her closet door and sifted through her clothes. She didn't have much, but my eyes landing on that damn pink dress she wore the first day of classes, but I pushed it aside. A brown dress that wrapped around itself caught my eye and I pulled it out, tossing it onto her bed.

"Change." I pointed as I left the bedroom and waited for her in the hall.

Thank goodness Jolee wasn't one of those high maintenance chicks. She was wearing the dress and a pair of heeled boots in five minutes flat. As she stepped out of her bedroom, she was twisting her long hair into a knot at the nape of her neck and I had to fight the urge to press my lips at the exposed skin.

"Is this suitable?" she asked as she did a little spin in front of me. I wanted to tell her that she was perfect before, and even more perfect naked and spread out on the bed, but I bit my tongue and nodded instead.

"Let's go," I growled and trudged toward her door; she followed, grabbing her coat and bag along the way.

"Hey guys," she said as she closed her apartment door to find Archer and Link standing in the hallway. She smiled at them warmly, fucking smiled, and I wanted to beat my brothers' faces in as they returned it.

"I thought we were in a hurry, Link," I bellowed, pulling Jolee's arm and racing down the steps.

"I'm pretty sure she'll forgive us now."

Beside me, Jolee asked, "Forgive you for what?"

"For being an asshole," I told her, referring to Link.

In the parking lot, I shoved Jolee into my car before Link could suggest us all riding together in his Jeep. I wanted to make sure that when I was good and ready to leave that I could. As he tucked himself into his driver's seat, I could sense that Link knew exactly what I was doing. He shook his head with narrowed eyes, but really, what did he have to be upset about? He got me going to dinner even though there were far better things I wanted to do with my time – like the girl sitting next to me.

Cars scattered in the driveway of Tracy's house, and I made sure to park on the neighborhood street so that I didn't get blocked in when I was ready to leave.

"Ready?" I asked Jolee, who had remained quiet throughout the entire ride, her face turned toward the window.

"Ford, what am I doing here?"

"I didn't want you to be alone." She cocked one of her eyebrows, silently asking me to try again with the truth. "Maybe I didn't want to be alone," I answered honestly. I may be surrounded by a room of surrogate brothers, aunts, and uncles, but amongst them, I was just a buoy bobbing along in an ocean where I didn't belong.

"Okay." I was amazed at how easily Jolee accepted my answer. She didn't question, didn't fight, she reached over and opened her car door and stepped out while I stared at her in amazement.

She was going to make some lucky bastard very happy one day.

RENEE HARLESS

CHAPTER THIRTEEN

JOLEE

Ford had grabbed my hand the moment he exited his car. He seemed apprehensive about it, but couldn't help himself. Which just confused the heck out of me. There were times when I thought Ford and I were crossing a bridge together, trying to figure things out, but then we'd both pull back. It was that two steps forward, three steps back mentality. We both knew that we wanted each other, but we were both scared of what that meant; what we'd each have to give up for that kind of happiness. There were sacrifices I wasn't willing to make and I knew that Ford felt the same.

But as he intertwined our fingers together as we walked up the front steps, I really wished that we could figure things out. He looked handsome in an olive-green sweater that seemed just a bit too snug around his arms.

The front door opened by one of the other ridge rogues and I found myself trying to tug my hand back as I stepped inside the Colonial-style brick house, but Ford tightened his fingers around my hand.

His family seemed warm and welcoming as I was introduced and shown a seat at a huge dining table. All of the preparations were laid out family-style and I couldn't wait to dig in. Holidays were a small affair at the house where I grew up - if they happened at all.

Conversation flowed around the table, but whenever someone tried to engage with Ford, he gave a one or two-word answer before clamming up. Even sitting beside me he seemed uncomfortable, and I wasn't sure why.

"Do you want to leave?" I whispered to him just as desserts were passed around. Link was sitting on my other side and tensed up as I suggested our retreat.

"We can stay a little while longer," Ford murmured close to me.

"Okay." Reaching over, I gently squeezed his hand before diving into the apple pie and ice cream in front of me.

Regardless of how uncomfortable Ford seemed to be with all of the people in the room, I really took a liking to them. They were warm and loving – something I had been craving from my own family. Tracy was not only a phenomenal parent, she was a great human being as well. I could see the absolute love she had for each of her boys, and there was no doubt that they were hers. Love filled this home.

Tyler, the youngest and Ford's cousin, was hoping to attend Wellington University on a baseball scholarship, but I sensed that, like Ford, he was extremely bright. All of the brothers seemed to be — even Archer when he wasn't messing around. I had a feeling that he used his looks and humor to mask how smart he was.

When Ford and I left, the brothers waved goodbye, but Tracy wrapped me in her arms and I could completely sense that she felt as if she was adopting me into her family. Something about her wanted you to feel accepted.

I wasn't sure if Ford held the door open for me out of chivalry or because Tracy was standing at the door watching, but I made sure to thank him anyway.

"You have a really great family, Ford. Thank you for letting me be a part of it today."

He didn't answer. Instead, he turned the key in the ignition and pulled away from the neighborhood.

We were about five minutes down the road when I turned in my seat, irritation simmering on the surface. "You know what? You really confuse me, Ford."

"I know," he murmured beside me.

"Do you? Because one minute you want me, and the next you don't. Then you go off in the middle of something, probably for another girl. And now here I am having a holiday meal with your family. I don't know which way is up with you, Ford."

"I know, Jolee, okay? I get it."

We sat in silence for the remainder of the drive. I nervously toyed with the hem of my dress, wondering what the hell I was doing. I sat here with a boy that seemed to have his mind focused on something else almost all of the time. The only time he gave anything his full attention was when we were fighting or in bed together. Neither of those was how I wanted to live my life, except I had no power of refusal against Ford. He had morphed into my Achilles' heel at some point this semester.

"Please just drop me off."

"Okay," he replied, but I could tell he was growing tense at my request.

The car pulled to the curb and I turned in my seat to look at the lonely boy that had become an expert at pushing people away.

"I. . .I'm going to need you to leave me alone, Ford," I told him as I shut the door.

I didn't expect him to follow me, maybe a mean comment or two because that was what Ford and I did, but he wasn't the type of person to chase.

The moment I stepped into my apartment, I kicked off my boots and ripped the dress from my body, throwing it on the floor. I didn't want to look at it for at least another twenty-four hours. In my room, I grabbed my bathrobe, wrapped it around myself, and sat at my desk. Winter break was coming soon and I was too angry to consider spending it here, alone, again. So, I found myself looking up plane tickets to Alaska. My parents wouldn't be there, but at least it would be home.

My search for flights turned into researching seven-day cruises to the Bahamas and I wasn't sure exactly how much time had passed until a knock on the apartment door sounded. I glanced at the clock on the lower corner of my computer screen and realized that a full hour had passed.

The knocking repeated and I trudged from my bedroom to the door, peering through the peephole before opening it just a crack.

"What are you doing here, Ford?"

The devilishly handsome man ran a hand through his messy mane and I had to force myself not to swoon. He had a pull on me that I couldn't ignore, no matter how much I tried.

"I don't know," he said, seeming both frustrated and sincere. Maybe he felt the same pull that I did.

"If you don't know, then why are you standing at my door? I'm tired, Ford. Tired of games, hell, I've been playing them too, but I just. . . I don't need it. I have other things to worry about."

"God, Jolee, don't you see? I'm tired too, so fucking tired of fighting the thing I have for you even though I know that I have zero things to offer."

I leaned against the door jamb, the lapels of my robe slipping open, exposing the crevice of my breasts. "You have a lot of things to offer, Ford, you are just. . .preoccupied."

He seemed to deflate at my words and I wondered if everything he had mentioned about his father was what kept him at a distance from everyone. I couldn't imagine how much time or energy it took to hate someone so much.

"You're right," he said, surprising me. "I have a lot of things going on right now, but I'm selfish, so fucking selfish, Jolee."

The thing was, I was selfish too. Dumb, weak, and selfish, and I wanted Ford even though we were in two different places. He thought I was altruistic, but when it came to him, I was the complete opposite.

Reaching out, I grasped his hand and pulled him into my apartment knowing that I was being so foolish, but I couldn't stop. I came to Wellington to make a change in my life, that included being a reckless girl.

Ford and I spent the entire Thanksgiving holiday in my bed, only leaving for takeout delivery and other necessities, but for the most part, we stayed in my room. Ford ran to his apartment early yesterday morning to grab a pair of sweatpants but was back before I even realized that he had left.

He was already moving around in my kitchen, leaving my bed cold and empty, but unlike before, I could hear him loud and clear destroying our apartment. Pots and pans banged and clanked, the sounds vibrating all the way to my room.

Lazily I made my way toward the kitchen, twisting my hair into a messy knot on the top of my head. But as I reached the kitchen, my eyes zeroed in on Ford and almost bulged out of the sockets. He was standing bare-chested at my stove, appearing to poach some eggs, while wearing sweatpants. Not just any sweatpants, but well-worn gray sweatpants that hung low on his hips. From behind, the two dimples just above his backside called out to me and I wanted desperately to reach out and touch them. Then Ford turned around and I almost choked on my tongue. Outlined beneath the tattered cotton was his cock and I didn't think that I had ever seen something so glorious. Sure, I had seen Ford completely naked, but something about the sweatpants just enhanced the planes of his body.

"Hey, babe, you're just in time. I'm making eggs benedict."

I didn't focus on if we had the ingredients to make that sort of breakfast or how he even knew how to make it; I was focused on the fact that he called me babe.

"I think that's the first time you haven't called me princess," I told him as I wrapped my arms around his waist from behind and pressed my lips against his shoulder blade. His hair was damp from a shower that he must have taken and water dripped from the ends onto his skin.

Ford turned around and placed his hands on my jaw, tilting my face toward him. "I can go back to calling you that if you'd like."

"That's okay," I answered with a grin.

Leaning down, Ford sealed our lips together, and it was the most right anything had felt in a long time. The microwave on the counter beeped, but Ford didn't relent as his tongue stroked against mine.

It wasn't until a coughing noise resonated in the living room that we jumped apart.

"Willow!" I exclaimed, startled by my roommate's early appearance, but she was focused on the man who had gone back to plating our breakfast.

"Seriously, I want all of the details," she said, not caring in the slightest that Ford was standing beside me.

"How about some breakfast first?" he asked her and I had to force myself not to walk over to her and cover her eyes as he turned around and sat my plate on the counter. I knew that she was checking out all of the goods on display. And I couldn't even blame her.

She finally seemed to understand what he had asked and she shimmied onto the barstool next to me and nodded. "I will take you up on that offer, kind sir. And if you keep this up, you are welcome here any time."

Ford seemed happy with her declaration as he reached over and pressed his lips against mine once more.

"I'm going to let you guys eat. I probably need to let Link know I haven't died."

"Don't you want something to eat?"

"Naw, I have a brand new box of my favorite snack since someone stole it a few weeks back."

My cheeks reddened knowing that he knew I stole his bag of Cookie Crisp, but he had deserved it. I was a bit surprised that he was just getting around to replacing it.

"What have you been eating since then?"

"I stole Archer's Captain Crunch." Ford went to my bedroom and gathered his things before heading to the apartment door. "See you tomorrow."

"Bye."

I turned back toward my delicious breakfast, still in awe that Ford made something like this in a college apartment kitchen, but mostly trying to ignore Willow's stare penetrating the side of my face.

"Oh girl, you are in so much trouble."

After the break, most of the classes on campus didn't start up again until Tuesday, so I was given an additional day of reprieve away from Ford.

I wasn't sure what Ford had anticipated after our weekend together. I wasn't assuming that we were a couple or anything, but some clarification would have been nice. I mean, if all he wanted was a girl to warm his bed at night, I wasn't completely opposed and would probably be the first in line.

Nevertheless, Ford and I were on two different wavelengths, pushing and pulling each other when we were close enough. I had slept with him more times than I had anyone else, but we hadn't even exchanged phone numbers. It was a strange situation that I wasn't ready to give up just yet. He was beyond addictive and I knew that my yearning for him stemmed from those small moments that he allowed me to see the secret side of him, to hear the parts of his dirty past. And I was stubborn enough to believe that I could cleanse him.

I mulled through my statistics homework left over from the weekend, then trudged my way across campus to the clinic. Dr. Allen was the veterinarian on duty and she was my favorite with whom to work. I ran through the first half of tasks making sure the animals were fed and the cages and kennels were clean.

"Jolee, the patient in room two, is insisting that you be present," one of the technicians called out. I scurried from the cat room and made my way to the front examination rooms. It wasn't completely unheard of for patients to request a staff member in the room with the doctor, but I hadn't been working here long enough to have those sorts of requests yet.

Dr. Allen was reading through the patient's file – a blue tab on the bottom indicated that they were a new cat – I stood beside her patiently.

"So, you have a new cat?" Dr. Allen asked as she entered the room. I walked in behind her.

"You may leave," the dark voice growled and Dr. Allen stopped abruptly.

"Excuse me?" she asked firmly.

"I have things to discuss with your employee."

Dr. Allen glanced back at me and I caught my first glimpse of Rutherford Hastings standing beside an empty animal carrier. The blood drained from my face as he sneered in my direction.

"I don't think so, Mr. Hastings."

"Senator," he bellowed, but Dr. Allen wasn't fazed.

"If you need to speak with Ms. Ward, you may do so in my presence, that is if she wants to speak to you at all."

"If she wants a grant for her animal rescue, she better be prepared to listen to every single word that I have to say."

Dr. Allen cautiously stepped aside but made sure that she was close enough to me to pull me out of the room if necessary. She was aware that anything involving my rescue was of the utmost importance to me, even if it was coming from the threatening senator.

I crossed my arms against my chest and stared him down. I was not going to show how intimidated I felt by him. "Say what you want, then leave."

"This is a check for five million dollars — more than enough to open your rescue. In return, I want you to give me the information that my *consequence* has gathered. He thinks he is so sly, but I've been tracking him since the day he was born."

"What makes you think that I have any idea what you're talking about?" I asked exasperatedly.

"Because I've watched you with him and you know deep inside that there is something he is hiding." Disgusted shivers traveled down my spine at his insinuations and the thought of him spying on me with his son didn't sit well with me.

"What happens if I don't?"

"I'll make sure that your rescue never sees the light of day." He slid the check across the stainless steel counter until it was within my reach and I found myself staring at it. I had never seen so many zeroes in real life. "I'm just going to leave this with you. Mail the information to the address in the corner. You have two weeks."

And just as quickly as he barged into my life, he disappeared, that was another thing that he had in common with his son.

I knew I wasn't going to take the money, but my biggest fear was that Senator Hastings was going to stop at nothing when it came to Ford.

How did I get tangled up in this mess?

The door slammed as he exited and I reached over to grab the check with a shaking hand.

"Shred this, please," I said to Dr. Allen as I handed the check to her.

"What is going on, Jolee? Are you in trouble?" she asked, taking the slip of paper from my hand.

"I'm not, but a friend of mine may be. Hastings doesn't scare me. I'm just not sure how far he is willing to go to get what he wants."

"Jolee, I don't like this at all. You don't come or leave without a ride, understand?"

"Yes, ma'am," I said as I exited the room to continue my work wondering if or how I would explain this run-in to Ford. He seemed to have so much on his plate regarding his mother that it seemed almost inconsequential to burden him with one more thing.

One of the technicians drove me to the shelter for my volunteer work and Ken waited while I called a rideshare home that night. I couldn't remember what had gone on most of that evening, my confrontation with Hastings running through my mind the entire time. The man was a creep, for sure, and I began to imagine that even though I didn't know Ford's mother, he seemed like someone that would have manipulated her. There was no way that she was naïve enough to think he was a good man. But then again, he was probably good at getting what he wanted, just like his son.

RENEE HARLESS

CHAPTER FOURTEEN

FORD

For two people that wanted no strings attached, Jolee and I couldn't seem to stay away from each other. She tried to ignore me in class, but that just left me egging her on as I had the first few weeks in economics. One morning I had pissed her off so bad that she shoved me into a storage closet while leaving the class to give me a piece of her mind, while I gave her mine. I had turned her around to face the sink and buried myself between her legs. Jolee broke apart quicker than I had ever seen. Whatever tension we had between us before seemed to melt away.

From that day forward, I made sure that she had my number and I walked with her to classes when I was able. Most of the student body thought we were together, but Jolee and I both knew that this was nothing more than sex, even if feelings were starting to evolve. We both had things that needed our attention.

We were insatiable for each other, even if we fought against it. She would text me to pick her up from the animal shelter and we would head to her bedroom or mine. My favorite part was the nights I would bypass our apartments all together and drive her to a secluded park. She would pretend to be angry because she was tired, but she would rid us of our clothes faster than I could put the car in park.

I feared that I was falling hard for her and I couldn't do anything to stop it, which meant she was going to find herself wrapped up in the mess that was my life.

Brent had been calling me almost on the hour with updates on documents he found related to my mother and my aunt and uncle. And his new intel claimed to find social worker documents where they manipulated the system to keep any family from adopting me.

I was leaving my last class of the afternoon heading back for my apartment when my phone rang in my pocket. Brent's name flashed across the screen and I quickly answered.

"Hey, man," I greeted.

"Hey. Can you meet me? I have some things to share with you."

"Sure, where at?"

It was late, but I still had a few hours before I needed to pick up Jolee.

"How about Anthony's Steakhouse across town? That way you're away from the school."

I calculated the distance and drive time then agreed to the meet up. I texted my brothers that I wasn't going to be at dinner as I made the trek across town. Anthony's Steakhouse was in a suburban area and as I pulled into the parking lot a few families shot worried looks as I exited the car. Brent was already seated and the hostess directed me to his table.

"Good to see you," I told him genuinely and he returned my welcome with a smile of his own.

"I'm going to treat you to dinner first, then we can get into the dirt. You look like you could use a few hours to relax."

He wasn't wrong. Things with Jolee were moving faster than I knew possible and worry for my mother continued to escalate daily. Jolee had been acting a little differently, but I assumed it was the pressure of final exams.

I wasn't in a good place mentally or physically. And truthfully, I was damn tired. Tired of fighting, tired of feeling worthless, tired of acting like I had my shit together.

Brent and I both ordered a steak and potato, killing time by talking about crazy things he saw when he was on the force. He and Adam went on the craziest calls. I remember that Adam once told me that they were called to a house fire that belonged to a hoarder who had chained himself to the porch because he didn't want to leave his things.

Brent also asked me about Meredith, seeming happy when I told him that she had taken a liking to Nathan. He wanted my mother free almost as much as I did.

As the server took away our meals and gave us each a refill on our beers, Brent pulled out a new manila envelope.

I slipped my finger beneath the flap and pulled out the photocopies.

"Let me preface this by saying I have lead on a reporter that will text me when they are available to run the story. "

"So, you found it?" I asked enthusiastically.

"That and more.

"First, you'll find paperwork from the hospital detailing that your mother is of right mind. And the night you were taken, she passed the psychiatric evaluation. The next document shows that your birth father had a new doctor who had not seen your mother forge documents to have her committed without a chance of appeal. Those first documents were never stored electronically and had been in the hospital's warehouse. Hastings must have assumed that no one would go looking for them.

"Under the second paperclip, you'll find documents with your father's official letterhead threatening blackmail against the authorities that arrested your mother and the judges in the district where she would stand trial. Your mother had no chance to have any trial turned over. It also shows that your father kept a tight leash on your whereabouts, forcing social workers to put you into the foster care system instead of with family."

"I can't believe it. I knew he was vile, but this is. . ." I said, my words trailing off in disbelief.

"Really, this isn't even the worst I've found when I started researching him, and unfortunately, your mother isn't the only one he has duped and done horrendous things to. If you go ahead with the reporter, your mother won't be the only one mentioned.

"That being said, the third set of documents relate to your aunt and uncle. My intel traced conversations that were held from your father's office phone, where he sought out a hitman. They were asked to create a believable car accident that would be sure to end both lives. Your cousin was very lucky not to have been in the car that night. Your father figured that the child was too young to ask questions as they had."

"So he murdered my aunt and uncle," I whispered, not wanting to draw the attention of the patrons sitting around us.

"I wish I had another answer for you, but yes. Yes, he did."

"God, I'm going to kill him," I seethed as I pushed out of the booth. Brent reached out and grabbed my arm.

"Sit down, Ford. There is something else I need to show you." He waited until I was sitting back on the bench before pulling out another paper with a collage of pictures. "Remember when I told you to watch out for yourself?" When I nodded, he continued. "You need to do the same for your girl."

Brent flipped the paper around toward me and I was left staring at pictures of Jolee and me. Some around campus, some outside of the apartment, and a few of her by herself at work. I had been furious before, but now I was livid. He was hell-bent on destroying everything good in my life.

This time Brent stood from the booth, leaving the compilation of pictures laid out in front of me. One of his rugged hands landed on my shoulder and I looked up at him warily. "Be careful, Ford. I'm not sure that this is the worst Hastings is capable of. I'll text you when the reporter is ready."

He squeezed my shoulder as he left and I sat in place staring at the information that could destroy my father, but I wasn't as confident as I had been before. It was almost like gathering the information had been fun, but now that vengeance was within my grasp and I wasn't sure that it was so sweet. Regardless of my feelings, though, I needed to make a statement and my father needed to go down. A taste of his own medicine was the only way that I knew how.

The waitress came by once more to ask if I needed anything and I found myself gathering up the materials quickly so that she didn't catch a glimpse of the pictures or papers. I shoved them into my bag and left the restaurant.

The knowledge of what I carried with me possessed me to drive to one of the harbor overlooks. I took a turn into a well-off neighborhood and drove to the large brick estate at the end of the road.

Lights shone on the mansion, illuminating its red exterior in the darkness of the night. Without a second thought, I parked the car, left the engine running, and made my way up the stone path to the front door. Not bothering with the doorbell, I pounded the side of my fist against the door.

It swung open as a tall thin man answered and asked how he could help me.

"I want to speak to my sperm donor," I commanded and the man's face paled. I knew he was taken aback by my words and appearance, but there was no denying the Hastings' eyes. Just then, my father turned the corner appearing as if he was readying to leave. Instead of paling like his hired help, Hastings stomped toward the front door and pushed me from the entrance.

"Stay away from here, boy."

"No, you stay away. Stay away from me, stay away from my mother, and stay away from Jolee."

He had the audacity to chuckle at my exclamation, which only fired me up more.

"At least you got your good taste from me."

"You're disgusting, old man. You may be able to fool everyone around you, but you can't fool me. I'm going to destroy you."

"Oh yeah? And how are you going to do that? No one is going to believe a word that you say, not against mine."

"Don't you worry your empty head about that, old man. Just know that it's coming."

"Rutherford," a voice called out from inside the house and my sperm donor answered, "I'm coming."

Turning his attention to me once more, he added, "I'm not afraid of you, boy."

"Yes you are, I can see it in your eyes. And you should be, your time is up."

"Is it? Maybe it's your time that is up. How do you know that I won't set my eyes on taking you out?"

"You could, but you won't," I tell him as I make my way down the steps back to my car.

"What makes you say that?"

"You've had twenty-two years to end my existence, but you haven't. Because all it would take is a DNA test or a look at my birth certificate to prove that I was your son, you'd be the first suspect." I opened the door to my car and leaned over the hood addressing my father for the last time. "Your run is up, Senator Hastings."

I flew out of his driveway, my tires squealing as I left him standing in the porch light's illumination. I had no destination in mind as my heart pounded, then signs for the water overlook drew my attention and I exited off the main road.

I turned the ignition off and watched the boats bob in the dark sea, their red and green lights flashing against the waves.

I wondered what my mother's life would have been like if she hadn't gotten pregnant with me, or had decided to end the pregnancy. Would she have finished law school and moved across the country as she had planned? Or would she have been buried under Hastings' thumb still? Would she have been happy? Married? Had other kids? I couldn't stop the questions from flowing until I was bursting at the seams with them.

My hands reached into my hair as I tugged at the ends hating the guilt that rose through me, knowing that I was the reason my mother had her life destroyed. It was all my fault. All the bad things in my mother's life were because of my existence and she barely had me long enough to witness any of the good.

The one thing I knew, though, was that my mother loved me unconditionally. She told me every time I called, every time I visited. I couldn't imagine having been in her shoes – having your young child taken from you for no reason and then having zero contact for another few years. My mother and I were both lucky that I had been given to Tracy.

Glancing over to my bag, I wondered what my cousin Tyler would think of all of this, of knowing that my birth father was the reason his parents had been killed. I wasn't even sure if I should tell him or simply let the report document the details, then maybe it would seem as if the reporter was the one that had done the digging, not me.

I wasn't sure how long I sat in my car captivated by the boats, but the chill from the winter air began to ooze into the vehicle. There was a snow storm on the horizon just as school was letting out for winter break. As I started the car, I thought about how I would spend my classes next semester without Jolee to torment. I suspected that we weren't going to be in any of the same courses. Good thing she lived the floor above me.

My back went ramrod straight at thoughts of Jolee. Fuck, I was supposed to pick her up from the shelter. Glancing down at my phone, I realized that I was already an hour late. I wasn't so worried that she was going to chew me out and most likely hold back from any sex for the night. I was afraid about Brent's threat – that my father may be watching her too. I sent her a text apologizing for not picking her up, but she only replied that she was home.

My car sped through the streets of Boston until I made it onto the Wellington campus, heading straight for the apartment complex. Grabbing my bag and keys, I took the stairs two at a time until I made it to the fourth-floor landing.

For some reason, I felt relief to find Jolee standing at the entrance to her apartment, waiting for me. She didn't look angry or upset, just. . .concerned.

"Are you staying or going?" she asked, tiredness evident in her voice. In the last two weeks, a purple and bluish tint had grown under her eyes. She was wearing thin.

"Staying, but just to sleep." We had been sharing a bed for so many weeks, I wasn't sure that I could sleep at night without her.

"Good, because I'm too tired for anything else," she said as she walked inside, assuming I would follow behind. I was sure to lock the apartment door and made my way to her bedroom.

Jolee had already laid herself on the side of the bed that she claimed, while I pulled out her desk chair and piled my things on the seat.

"Did you walk home?" I asked her as I finished laying my pants on the back of the seat and made my way toward the bed.

Her voice was heavy with sleep when she said, "No, I called a rideshare."

"Okay." I tugged the sheets aside and wrapped my arms around her waist; even though she didn't seem upset about the missed ride, she didn't seem like herself. I knew that she was self-sufficient. Hell, we were only having sex, but I would have thought she would have texted me as a reminder.

"Hey, Ford, don't forget that I'm leaving tomorrow."

Leaving? Where was she going? Something chimed in the back of my mind that she had mentioned something a few weeks back, something about Alaska.

Then it dawned on me. "You're going home for winter break. Right?"

"Yeah."

It was going to suck not having her here for a couple of weeks, but I'd cope. And knowing that I was going to have Brent reach out with the reporter at any time, it was probably better that she left anyway.

But still, I knew that I was going to miss her. And maybe, just maybe, I'd be able to salvage something with her when I destroyed my father's world.

CHAPTER FIFTEEN

JOLEE

The need to tell Ford about his father's threats had been weighing on me for days, but tonight it was what kept me tossing and turning in bed. I wasn't sure how he was going to take the news that his father had approached me and made idle warnings. Then again, I wasn't even sure if Ford would care. Most days, I didn't know where we stood. We would share a bed, and a few of our deepest desires and secrets, then we'd go all day without talking. I'm not sure if it was for any other reason than self-preservation.

One thing was clear, though, and it was that Ford's father knew how powerful he was and he was going to use that to keep me from getting everything I've worked for. My rescue was everything I had been dreaming of since I was in high school and I was about to lose it all over a fling with Ford.

Except when I thought about the way Senator Hastings was out to destroy his son's happiness, I felt overrun with anger. And I knew that my feelings for Ford were more than just something fun and flirty.

When he hadn't picked me up from the shelter, my first thoughts went to him being in trouble, but I had no way of knowing. Which only left me more anxious. My mind was so scattered that I hadn't thought to message or call him, and that was stupid on my part. Instead, I had rushed home hoping to find him at his apartment, but when I knocked on the door, Link told me that Ford was out having dinner with a friend.

I was calming down just as Ford sent a message apologizing and I replied to him that I was home. I took a shower and got ready for bed, working overtime to calm my nerves. When I heard the pounding of feet in the stairwell next to my bedroom, I subconsciously knew that it was Ford.

I rushed to the apartment door and opened it just as he had arrived on the landing. Seeing him unharmed as he came up the stairs, with his own look of relief on his face, was enough to calm me.

And then my exhaustion hit. I wanted nothing more than to sleep wrapped in a blanket of Ford, even if I knew the guilt at omitting his father's visit was going to keep me awake. I had my reasons – mostly that I wanted Ford to stay focused on school until the end of the semester.

Just as I tried to doze off, I reminded him that I was leaving tomorrow, which he seemed to forget. I had decided that a break from him and Wellington would probably be good for me, even knowing that my parents wouldn't be home. It wasn't like we had celebrated Christmas before. Most of the holiday was spent on a research trip, and when I got older, I spent it at home alone or with a neighbor.

Willow was excited that I was going home and offered to travel with me despite the fact that she hated crowds, airports, and planes. But I declined her suggestion.

I stared at the orange glow coming from the lamppost outside the complex as it filtered between the horizontal blinds on the window. Reaching out, I flipped over my phone to view the time, 5 a.m., and I hadn't slept a wink. Ford had moved onto his back, one muscled arm draped over his head while the other rested against his stomach.

I sat up slowly and tried to get my eyes to adjust to the room, but other than the soft glow, the room was washed in darkness. Above my head, I stretched my arms and twisted my waist until my feet hit the floor.

Since I was awake, I figured I might as well get the day started. I moved around the bed until my foot collided with a heavy boot, causing me to trip and fall into my desk chair that somehow was moved into the center of the walkway. The fall into the chair caused me to reach my arm out to catch myself and I found my hand colliding with the cold metal and plastic of my laptop. None of my reactions kept me from falling onto the floor on my backside, with the chair falling on top of me.

"Cheese and rice!" I cried out when I fell with a crash.

"Jolee! Are you okay?" Ford asked as he flipped on the lamp beside him.

"Yeah," I told him as I moved the chair upright and piled his clothes back onto the seat. "I'm okay. Just tripped, that's all."

Turning onto my knees, I lifted my laptop off the ground and placed it back on my desk, praying that I would be able to salvage it. Then I reached for a pile of papers scattered across my floor that were spilling out from Ford's bag.

I lifted the first paper-clipped stack without a second glance, but then Ford jumped from the bed, sliding in front of me to gather the rest of the papers. That was when I decided to look down at what I held in my hand. It shook as I read through the document related to Meredith O'Brien's arrests and psychiatric evaluations. Glancing up at Ford, I noted the shame covering his face. His eyes were downcast and his chin tilted toward his chest. I flipped the page and found more information about his mother and forged documentation, locking her in a facility.

I knew what I was holding in my hands, but I didn't want to believe it. He couldn't have stooped this low. Was this what his father had been talking about and I guilelessly told him that Ford wasn't up to anything?

But then anger welled up inside of me, threatening to drown me in fury. This was what he had been up to. What had kept him at arm's length. What kept him from experiencing the love that his family wanted to share with him.

"I want to see them," I growled, holding out my hand for the other sheets he collected.

"No, Jolee." He sounded fatigued, but not in the sense that he was tired, but that he had no more fight left.

"Show me, Ford."

Cautiously he handed the second and third stack into my palms. Letters about blackmail, deceit, and murder lined the pages. And there were roughly three hundred papers and pictures related to Ford's mother, other women, and Ford's aunt and uncle. I had a very bad feeling about the things he had discovered.

I looked up at him again, anguish painted in his eyes and mouth, while he held one last paper to his chest.

"Ford. . ." I said, gesturing for him to give me the additional piece of paper.

Slowly he flipped the paper over and showed it to me, still afraid to lay it in my grasp.

"Is that. . .?" I asked as I leaned closer. They were pictures of me with Ford, several of them, and some of me by myself or at work. Some were old and some were from a few days ago.

"What does this mean? What are these?"

"It's nothing," he replied as he tried to take the papers from my hands, but I gripped them firmly and held them to my chest.

"Don't you dare lie to me, Ford O'Brien. Is this the revenge you were hoping for against your father? Have you been compiling this stuff? Do you have any idea how dangerous that is?"

"How about one question at a time?"

I wasn't a violent person by nature, but I had never wanted to pound my fist into someone so much before.

"Don't you dare joke with me. Tell me what the heck is going on."

"Jolee, just leave it alone. It doesn't concern you."

I stood up abruptly, gathering all of the documents and pictures against my body.

"No, I will not leave this alone. I'm in those darn pictures and I want to know why. What have you done, Ford?" I was shouting now, most likely waking up my roommates, but I was done caring. I was probably going to need witnesses soon anyway with the violence I felt surging through me.

"Calm down, Jolee," Ford shouted back.

"Don't tell me to calm down! Is this why your father is trying to pay me off? Are these the things he wanted?"

Ford grew silent at my question and it took me a moment to realize what I had said.

"Ford, I-"

"What did you say about that waste of human existence?"

Admitting my omission, I told him, "Your father has come to me twice to find out what you had on him. Obviously, I told him I didn't know anything."

"What did he offer you?"

"Five million in grant money for my rescue in exchange for whatever you had found on him. I had the check shredded the moment he left."

"You should have taken it."

"Excuse me? I didn't know any of this existed," I said, shaking the papers in my hand. "But why does he even know about me? Tell me what all of this is, Ford. Why do you have it?"

Ford moved from the floor and onto the desk chair that looked minuscule beneath him.

"I hired a private investigator two years ago, someone that used to work with Tracy's husband. I knew that my mother had no reason to be in the facility where she lives; the workers even know that she's completely sane. And I knew *knew* that Hastings was the reason she was there. Then things spiraled out of control. I got more than I ever thought existed. I want vengeance for my mother and my family."

"But at what cost, Ford? What good is it going to do anyone to have this information?"

"My mother will be free. And my sperm donor's name will be thrown through the mud. I'm hoping he'll spend the rest of his days as someone else's bitch."

His eyes lit up as he spoke of revenge against his father, and for the first time, I didn't know or understand the boy sitting across from me.

"There is a reporter-" he began and I knew where he was going. I was filled with disgust. Pure unfiltered disgust.

"Ford, no. No, you can't go to a reporter with this."

He seemed puzzled as I shot him down, as if he didn't expect that reaction, especially knowing what I did about his father and mother.

"What do you mean? I have to, Jolee, don't you see? He'll never let my mother out of the facility and my cousin will live the rest of his life thinking his father was driving drunk and lost control of the car."

"Think of what will happen if you smear their names through the paper. This is not the way to go about it, Ford. You're going to ruin whatever happiness they've made with their lives. You have this illusion of a new reality, but that is never going to happen, Ford. You have to know that. Reporters aren't going to create the story that you want. They're going to create the story that they want to sell."

"You don't get it, Jolee. I have to exonerate my family."

"No, you know what you need to do?" I said, my voice rising with each second. "You need to grow the heck up."

His blue eyes iced over the same way that they had that first day we met, but I wasn't scared of him this time.

Beside me, Ford's phone pinged on the nightstand and I glanced over to see the name Brent on the screen.

Brent: Reporter at 7am

"The reporter will be ready at 7 a.m."

Ford nodded as he looked at me expectantly.

"You're going, aren't you?" I asked, already knowing the answer. He was willing to destroy his family all for some game he'd formulated in his mind. "Don't be the boy everyone believes that you are, be the man that I know you can be."

"You're not making sense."

"You know what? Take your freaking papers and make the worst decision of your life. And know that I warned you that your family will never forgive you for airing out everything this way. What's worse is that I don't think you even care." With a need to leave, I grabbed a pair of pants, slipping them over my shorts, and a sweatshirt from my dresser. I donned both in record time before slipping my feet into a pair of tennis shoes without any socks.

"Where are you going?"

"I'm leaving and I expect you gone when I get back."

"Jolee!" he shouted as I left my bedroom and headed down the hallway, surprised I didn't find my roommates waiting with bated breath in the hallway listening in. From behind he grabbed my elbow and spun me around. "What are you doing?"

"I'm leaving. I thought. . .you know, I thought that maybe you and I were going somewhere, Ford. Like we could discuss whatever this is between us. Maybe I was just a disillusioned girl wishing for a man to love her. I should have known better and stayed away from you like I kept telling myself. I can't forgive you for this. Your father is probably going to ruin my career and you're deadset on destroying everything. You're nothing more than a silly boy."

His jaw dropped at my rant and I left him staring at my back as I let myself out of the apartment. I had no destination in mind and found myself at a coffee shop on the edge of dark side before entering the school campus. Strangely I felt no remorse for the way I spoke to Ford because I was still in awe of what he planned to do. He was exactly as I had described: a silly boy.

I stayed at the coffee shop for an hour sipping on two chai tea lattes, lamenting at the loss of whatever it was that Ford and I had. I still wasn't quite sure, other than I was hoping that I could figure out a way to stay focused on my dreams and have him too. He made it clear that whatever we had was nothing and I needed to learn that it was okay. It simply reiterated the fact that I needed to remain alone.

I had to pack for my flight back to Alaska, not needing to bring much since I had left a lot of clothes at my parents' house, but I needed to bring the essentials.

Slowly I made the trek back to my apartment, hesitating as I opened the door. I didn't need to walk past the entryway to know that Ford had left, as I requested. I could always sense when he was close and now was no different.

"Oh my gosh, Jolee. What is going on?" Willow asked as she ran from her bedroom in alarm. "I saw Ford throw his things in a trash bag and leave, but I couldn't find you."

"I asked him to go."

"What? Why?"

"I don't want to talk about it, Willow. Not right now. I need to pack for my flight." I brushed passed her as I walked toward my bedroom, not intentionally trying to give her the brush off, but suddenly I felt more tired than I had ever been.

I tossed a few things into a carryon bag, never replacing the large suitcase that had broken my first day in Boston, and zipped it shut as I waited for Willow and Haley to walk with me toward the shuttle that would take me to the airport.

They both peppered me with questions about the fight that I had with Ford, but I wasn't sure what I could tell them. They would know soon enough though, whenever the paper or magazine ran the spread with Senator Hastings' demise.

"Are you sure you don't want to stay here? You'll be all alone up in Alaska."

Faking a smile, I sat my small piece of luggage on the ground with my bag carrying my laptop and wrapped my arms around her. "I'm used to being alone,

Willow. I'll be fine. Enjoy your break. You too, Haley," I added as I hugged my other roommate.

The shuttle arrived and I lifted both of my bags back into my grip and stepped inside the bus. From the window, I waved goodbye to my friends and hoped that some time away from Wellington University was the reset that I needed.

CHAPTER SIXTEEN

FORD

The plane bobbed in the air as it hit another wave of turbulence. I supposed that I deserved the horrendous flight after the way that I left things with Jolee. She had been right on all accounts. Right about me and right about Hastings.

Of course, Jolee was always right. I kind of loved that about her. And God, how I loved her. It took her walking away from me to realize that. But even then, I had been too stupid to do anything about it.

Looking off into the clouds surrounding the plane, I thought back to how everything led me to this moment.

I met with the reporter after Brent sent me a meeting place. A shrewd looking woman had waited in a black sedan as if we were going to exchange drugs and money, not throw Hastings to the wolves. I leaned into the car, the documents, emails, and pictures burning a hole through my clothes, and asked her why she wanted the assignment. I gave her credit for not lying. She told me that she had an act of revenge against Hastings herself. She wasn't interested in the politics and outrage that the article was going to cause, but she wanted vindication for her daughter.

I stood there listening to her explain her intentions of hiding our family name in the article, but I had an inkling that her editor would ask to disclose that information. She was placating me to get her information, but something held me back. That revenge I had felt for so long morphed into something else, something akin to protection. I needed to defend and guard my family against my father.

When I declined the reporter's offer, she was shocked at first and tried to persuade me once more, but ended up slipping me her card in case I changed my mind. I had no preconceived notions that this was the last time she or any reporter would approach me. Word would get out that I had information related to my father – the kind of dirt that would sell papers and magazines.

I walked back to my car and called Brent, explaining that I was grateful for the information he found, but that I couldn't go through with it. When he asked me why, I told him that the girl in the pictures had changed everything.

Instead of driving to my apartment, I drove toward Tracy's house knowing that it was early on a Saturday and Tyler would still be home. I needed to unload it all and figure out what my next steps were.

Tracy was in the kitchen making breakfast for her and Tyler when I walked into the house. I had texted my other brothers when I parked my car, hoping that they would arrive soon too.

"Hi, honey. This is an unexpected visit."

"Yeah, sorry I came unannounced," I told her as I kissed her cheek then moved to the table beside Tyler, dropping my bag on the table.

"You know that I'm always happy to have you. What brings you by?"

"I wanted to speak with everyone about something. Everyone else should be here soon."

"Okay. Can I make you something to eat while you wait?"

The thought of eating made me nauseous. I needed to get everything off my chest before I'd be able to taste anything real again.

It wasn't much longer when my brothers arrived, gladly accepting Tracy's offer for breakfast. They stared at me over their plates as they shoveled in the home-cooked meal while I stared blankly at the manila envelope I placed on the table. When Tracy took her seat next to mine, I unleashed everything.

I explained what I had been doing all these years, why I had seemed so distant, and why I never felt like I belonged in a happy home if my mother was taken away because of me. I showed them the documents I had about Tyler's parents, about the blackmails against law enforcement and the court system, and finally all the details about my mother.

The silence that had filled the room was deafening. I wanted someone to speak up, to ask questions, to do something. But everyone except Tracy sat through my ten-minute spiel with forks dangling halfway to their mouths.

"Let me get this straight," Archer asked, finally breaking the silence. "You have proof your father did all of those things? Like hard evidence?"

"Yes. And I don't know what to do."

"Dude, how could you keep this from us? We're your family."

"I'm so fucking disappointed in you, Ford. We could have been there for you through all of this."

"What were you thinking, man?"

Beside me, Tyler hadn't moved or said much and I wasn't sure if that was a good or bad thing. I glanced over at him and caught his eye.

"I'm sorry, Tyler."

"I'm still processing, man. But it's not your fault. I know that much. And. . .ugh. . .thank you for not going to the press with this."

Then it hit me how right Jolee had been. I had been so focused on righting all of the wrongs within my arm's reach that I couldn't see the destruction that would have been left in its wake. My body jolted at the realization that I needed to go to her – like being struck by lightning.

"I need to go," I exclaimed as I stood from my chair, the wooden legs scraping against the hardwood floors.

"Where are you going?" Tracy asked as I began sifting through the documentation.

"I made a mistake and I need to fix it."

"Oh, my boy. You didn't mess things up with that nice girl, did you?"

"Of course, I did. I always mess things up. She's the one that said I shouldn't have met with that reporter to begin with, and you see how well I listened?"

"She's a smart one. I liked her. You better fix this."

"I'm trying, but she's on her way home," I explained as I set a pile of papers in front of her.

"Where is home?" Tracy asked and Link chimed in with a laugh, "Alaska."

"Oh dear, Alaska? Well, you better go get my wallet, can't have you making that trip in coach."

"What?" I asked, completely confused at what was happening, and before I knew it, Tyler had handed Tracy her purse while Rylan had retrieved her laptop from the desk in the kitchen.

"Now, what part of Alaska?" She directed her question to Link, who informed her that Jolee lived outside of Anchorage. It began to irk me that he knew so much about the woman I was in love with.

"Okay, I have you booked on a flight leaving in three hours. You won't have time to pack any clothes, but I'm sure they have nice stores there. I had the boarding passes sent to your phone," she said just as my phone chimed in my pocket.

"Tracy, I-"

"As a mother, any kind of mother, we want to see our children happy. There was no denying that when she came into your life, you changed for the better. Now, be on your way."

I wasn't sure what to say or how to react, so I did the one thing I knew would mean the most to her. I walked around and wrapped my arms around her shoulders tightly. "Thank you, Mom."

"Oh. . .well. . .you're welcome."

Before leaving, I explained that I wanted to see if we could get my mom released from the facility. Tracy took the *paperwork I handed her and said she would head there the moment I left.*

Everyone began piling out of the house, including Tyler, who walked with me to my car. I was waiting for the outburst, the anger, the resentment, but he showed none of them.

"You know I didn't want to tell you," I made clear as we stood by my car.

"Yeah, I still need to process everything."

"It's okay to be mad at me. I get it."

"It may take me a while to wrap my head around everything. Just. . .be there for me, okay?" He reminded me so much of the little boy they had brought in the month after the accident. His grandparents could no longer handle his outbursts and Tracy was given temporary custody. He had taken a long time to warm to everyone.

"I will."

The plane jerked as its tires landed on the tarmac. I glanced out the window and the sun was shining brightly even though I knew this time of the year they only got a couple of hours of daylight.

Nervousness enveloped me as I exited the plane. What if she didn't want to see me? What if she told me to leave? I wasn't prepared for any of those scenarios. I wasn't even sure I knew exactly where she lived.

On my way to the airport this morning, Link had texted me her address listed in the computer database. I didn't want to know how many rules he broke to get that information.

I was still in shock at how easily my brothers had accepted everything that I told them this morning. While I was away, they were going to brainstorm a way to take down my father.

Near the parking area, I flagged down a taxi and read him the address Link had provided. There was still an hour to go before we reached my destination.

I messaged Link again, gave him the details of my journey, and asked if Tracy had made any ground on getting my mother released. My mom was going to be flabbergasted if she was set free and I wish that I was there for the moment. But I knew Tracy would make her feel at home.

I watched the large city give way to suburban developments and then that give way to fields and trees. During the journey, the taxi driver pointed out some moose that were gathered by a frozen lake. For some reason, I had imagined Alaska as this snowy, iced-over state covered in mountains. Instead, I'm rewarded with lush fields and large bustling cities. I was never that kid that paid much attention in geography class, far more interested in the geometry and calculus.

"We're about twenty-five minutes away." The driver peered over the back seat as he spoke. "What brings you our way?"

With a heavy sigh, I said, "A girl."

"Must be some girl."

And for the first time in more days than I could count, I smiled, because she wasn't just some girl – she was everything.

Another ping sounded from my phone and I found a message from Link with a newspaper article web address. That smile I had been wearing drained from my face with the rest of my coloring. I was scared to open it, fearful of what I would see. Did the reporter gather enough information to publish the article on her own?

Link sent another message telling me to read it.

I held my breath as I clicked the URL, worried that I had made this voyage to Alaska for nothing. In bold, bright red letters the headline read:

SENATOR HASTINGS DIES OF HEART ATTACK

Immediately I dialed Link's number and asked him if the article was real, that Hastings had indeed passed away overnight from a heart attack when he was with another one of his mistresses. Based on the timing, he must have snuck away after my visit. He wasted no time in confirming the information and that various news sources were running the story.

It made the moment the taxi driver pulled into the driveway of a small brick house that much sweeter. I tossed the cash that Tracy had handed me on my way out this morning to the driver and asked him to sit tight for a few minutes. If Jolee wasn't going to see me, I was going to need a ride to the closest hotel. But I hoped that she would at least hear me out.

I knocked on the front door, rocking back and forth on my feet in nervous anticipation. After a minute passed, I knocked again. It hadn't occurred to me that she might not be home.

"Fuck," I mumbled as I knocked on the door one last time, ringing the doorbell as well once I found it tucked behind a plant on the porch.

That's when I finally heard feet pounding against the floors inside.

Oh, God, this was it. I was more nervous now than I had been in my entire life.

The door opened just a crack at first and my name was a confused whisper coming from her lips, then she opened the door wide. And I knew, without a shadow of a doubt, that I was in love with this woman. My heart raced as I took her in, the bare skin of her toes to the long blonde tips of her hair. I wanted nothing more than to grab her right then and never let her go, but I knew that she would define my next move.

"What are you doing here?" she asked, the hint of an oncoming sob evident as her voice hitched.

"I couldn't do it. I couldn't give it to the reporter. You were right that my family didn't deserve it. Instead, I told my brothers everything."

"Oh, Ford." She sounded relieved as her body relaxed against the door. "I'm really happy to hear that."

"My father died. Last night with his mistress," I informed her as I took out my phone and flipped it around for her to see the article that I still had pulled up.

"I'm sorry to hear that."

"Don't be, I'm not. That bastard deserved a far worse death than what he got. It also means that, with Tracy's help, my mother is free. That's all I wanted for so long, until now." I turned and held up a finger to the taxi driver to ask him to continue waiting as I stepped into Jolee's home, hoping that she wouldn't throw me out. "I came all this way not to tell you that I realized you were right or to beg you to come back to Wellington with me, but because I needed you to know that I'm in love with you."

"What?" she murmured, tears materializing along her lower lids.

Reaching a hand up to touch her cheek, I caressed the soft skin as I repeated, "I love you, Jolee Ward. You make me want to be the man that you deserve."

A watery smile grew on her lips just before she launched herself at me. I caught her easily, just as I always would. "I love you too, Ford.

"When I arrived this morning, everything felt wrong. This isn't my home anymore; all that is left here are bad memories. I want to be with you. I was on the phone trying to get a ride to the airport to go back to Boston."

"You were coming back to me?"

"Yeah, I was," she replied as she pulled back to look up at me.

"God, I love you," I told her before I kissed her lips with everything that I had. All of the love I felt bursting inside.

A few minutes passed where Jolee and I were attached at the mouth and if it weren't for the taxi driver honking at us, I probably would have stripped her bare right then and there.

"Get your things. You're coming back with me."

"Sir, yes, sir." She fake saluted me, which earned her a smack on her perfect ass. Pulling away, Jolee turned around to put her socks and boots on which had been resting against the wall. Her small piece of luggage and a bag was perched as if she was preparing to leave.

"Do you need to say goodbye to your parents?"

"I'll call them. They weren't going to be home anyway."

"Ready?" I asked her as I grabbed her suitcase and held out my hand for hers.

"Yes, more than ready."

Jolee sat next to me on the small couch as I watched my grown brothers tear into their Christmas gifts like a gathering of kindergarteners. Wrapping paper and bows were flying in all directions around the room. I hadn't touched a single one because I had everything I wanted sitting next to me.

"Will you open your darn gifts already?" Jolee said as she lightly smacked my arm and I rubbed it as if it had wounded me.

"I don't need any gifts."

"Well, maybe I want to watch you open them. Please?" she asked and I couldn't bear to tell her no. Her parents hadn't even called to wish her a Merry Christmas; they barely acknowledged her voicemail that she had returned to Boston. But Jolee wasn't letting any of that get her down. She seemed elated to spend the holiday with Tracy and my family. Last night she had told me that she had never had a big celebration and was excited to witness it.

We had been staying at Jolee's apartment since we arrived because none of her roommates were home, but I had already started looking at a place for both of us, even if we wouldn't be able to move in until summer. And since I was graduating this year, I needed to start researching jobs, at least until Jolee could open up her rescue. I planned to work beside her for the rest of my days.

Across from us, Meredith and Nathan sat together on the hearth in front of the fireplace. Her release hadn't happened immediately like I had hoped, but with my father's passing and the information that I had, the courts released my mother from the facility a few days later. She looked happier than I had seen my entire life. Meredith had seen the paperwork I had left with Tracy, and at first, she was angry, but the moment she was released from that building, she had let it all go. Like the sun had cleansed her of her anger and hate.

Women from all over the country had started coming out of the woodwork with their own stories against Hastings. At first, I felt terrible for his wife, children, and grandchildren, but from some of the articles I had seen, they weren't all that surprised. The country was turning against his memory faster than an ice cube melting in a flame. I asked Meredith if she planned on coming forward, but she smiled and told me that she was perfectly content with how things had turned out. As long as I was alive and thriving, she never needed to bring more despair to his family.

Right now my mother was staying with Tracy until she could figure out her next move, but I hoped that she and Nathan would find the love that I felt for Jolee, if they hadn't already.

With another push from Jolee, I moved to the floor to sift through my gifts. I wasn't as enthusiastic as my brothers, but it was fun to tear through the wrapping paper. Once we had opened all of the presents, I grabbed all of the discarded paper and carried it to the garage, but I did it under false pretenses.

With Tracy's help, I had a gift for Jolee that I knew she'd love.

"Come on, buddy," I said to the black and white Border Collie mix missing an eye. It was one of the puppies from the shelter that Jolee had always given a bit of extra love, and when I called yesterday morning, the puppy was still available. Tracy went to pick him up and grabbed a bunch of supplies. "Are you ready to meet your mommy?"

The puppy wagged his tail in excitement as I placed the red bow on his collar and lifted him out of the crate. Carefully I carried him through the mudroom until we came to the kitchen. I set him down on the floor and the little rascal took off toward the voices.

By the time I made my way into the living room, Jolee was scooping up Balboa (that was the name I had given him since Jolee and I bonded over our night with Rocky) into her arms and kissing his head.

"Merry Christmas," I whispered to her as I sat back beside her on the couch, Balboa squirming in her hands.

"I love him so much," she cried as she held him to her chest. She reached out to read his name tag and looked over at me with questioning eyes.

"Balboa, for Rocky," I explained.

"It's perfect. Thank you. I'm sorry that I didn't get you a gift. This was sort of unexpected."

"Believe me, I have the best gift of all."

And as Jolee settled against me with Balboa nestled across our legs, I knew that I really did have the best gift of all, the gift I had been searching for my entire life – my family. It wasn't conventional, but it was perfect. It just took this girl with broken luggage to open my eyes.

EPILOGUE

The spring sun was shining brightly in Boston this morning, melting the last bit of winter's snow. I was up early to help my brother, Ford, and his girlfriend, Jolee, set up a fundraiser at the local animal shelter down the road from Wellington University. This was where she had volunteered her time outside of classes and her job at the veterinary clinic. I didn't know how she found the time or energy to do any of this – she amazed not only me but all of the ridge rogues.

"Hey, where do you want this?" I asked Jolee as I carried the parts of the dunk tank. She had asked us all to volunteer our time this Saturday without any qualms, mainly because she knew we would say yes. For how she was able to save our brother from himself, we would do whatever she wanted. Plus, we all loved animals.

"Over by the big oak tree." She pointed in the direction she wanted across the front lawn.

I carried the large contraption over to the oak tree and sat it in the shade. People were already starting to arrive just as the workers at the shelter began carrying some of the dogs outside. They were the ones eligible for adoption. Ford was going to have his hands full trying to keep Jolee from bringing another pet home – they were still working on house training their puppy Balboa.

Glancing around the yard, I noticed a hose tucked around the side and went to grab it to start filling the dunk tank. Ford struggled to carry a few blowers for the bounce house and inflatable slides, and I was very tempted to turn the hose on him but held myself back. I didn't need Jolee coming after me. She may be beautiful, but she had a vicious tongue.

By lunchtime, the parking lot was filled and there were lines of students waiting to dunk volunteers in the tank or wait for food from a local food truck.

Knowing that my chance to grab a bite to eat was shrinking by the second, I made my way to the food truck and waited in line, pulling the brim of my hat down low.

Behind me, a soft voice rang out as she bumped into my back. "I'm sorry."

I turned around to tell her that it was fine, but my tongue caught in my throat. Her red hair hung down in soft waves around her face and her pale skin shone under the sun. But it was her brown eyes that held me captive. They reminded me of someone so familiar, someone I hadn't thought of for over ten years. The woman reached out to touch me and then suddenly I was transported back in time.

I shivered in the cold, dank apartment. The walls were peeling away and the floor felt wet beneath my feet. I sat on the couch, one of the springs poking into my thigh as I held tightly to the only picture we had of my parents.

The phone in the kitchen kept ringing, but I was scared to answer it. I was afraid it was my teacher calling to yell at me again. She didn't like how I acted in school and how I never turned in any homework, but I didn't have anyone to help me.

My parents left for a trip one day and never came back, my sister, Natalie, told me that they went to be with the angels. She packed me up in the small car my mother used and we moved into this nasty apartment that smelled like old people.

I hadn't seen my sister in three days and I hadn't left the apartment to go to school because I was afraid I wouldn't have a place to come back to.

Just as the phone stopped ringing, my sister stumbled into the apartment. I rushed to her and wrapped myself around her legs, but she kicked me away. Her red hair that had reminded me of Clifford the Dog had turned a weird color since my parents left, it was more like straw now. I didn't like it. I didn't like how her arms had bruises all over them, either.

"Sissy?" I asked as I scrambled onto my feet. My stomach had been growling for two days and all I had to eat was cereal. I hoped that she came home with more food because we didn't have anything left.

My sister bypassed me and went to the room we shared, ignoring me completely, as she slammed the door closed.

I counted as high as I could before I knocked on the door again, but my sister didn't answer.

"Natalie?" I called out as I peeked through a crack in the door.

She was draped halfway on the bed and halfway off like I did when I was dreaming about fighting bad guys.

"Sissy?" I said as I walked closer to her and rocked her shoulder with my hand. Usually, she would move or try to shove me away, but she didn't do any of those things.

"Sissy, wake up. My school keeps calling and I'm hungry."

I repeated the same motion until I rocked her so hard that she fell off the bed.

But she didn't do anything. She just laid there.

I knew what that meant. I had seen it on television when Natalie had stayed out late one night.

"Sissy!!!!!"

"Oh. . .um. . ," she murmured, breaking me free from my flashback.

I was glad that she had taken two large steps back because I was completely disgusted with myself and needed to find an escape.

"Hey, guys," Jolee said as she approached.

"I'm sorry, but I need to go," I told her without a backward glance.

And I just prayed that I didn't run into anyone as I sprinted home to burn my skin under the hot water.

It had been years since I had felt this dirty, this unglued. Leave it to a gorgeous redhead to bring my haunted past into the present.

CONTINUE READING THE RIDGE ROGUES IN
OF BISHOPS AND PAWNS

STAY IN TOUCH

Newsletter: http://bit.ly/2WokAjS
Author Page: www.facebook.com/authorreneeharless
Reader Group: http://bit.ly/31AGa3B
Instagram: www.instagram.com/renee_harless
Bookbub: www.bookbub.com/authors/renee-harless
Goodreads: http://bit.ly/2TDagOn
Amazon: http://bit.ly/2WsHhPq
Website: www.reneeharless.com

ACKNOWLEDGEMENTS

Thank you to all of the readers and bloggers that shared their excitement for this book and series. I have been waiting for years to share it with you and you've patiently waited for it to drop into your hands. I hope that it didn't disappoint.

Patricia, Lisa, Amanda R., Sally, Crystal, Amanda A, and Kelli thank you all so much for your help in making this book the best that it could be.

To the readers, this book has absolutely been one of my most favorite to write. I have a deep connection with Jolee and Ford and I hope that after reading their story that you will as well.

To my family, thank you for the weekends I had to lock myself away to give Ford and Jolee some attention, all while we lived during one of the most interesting times in our lives. I love you all so much, every day.

ABOUT THE AUTHOR

Renee Harless is a romance writer with an affinity for wine and a passion for telling a good story.

Renee Harless, her husband, and children live in Blue Ridge Mountains of Virginia. She studied Communication, specifically Public Relations, at Radford University.

Growing up, Renee always found a way to pursue her creativity. It began by watching endless runs of White Christmas- yes even in the summer – and learning every word and dance from the movie. She could still sing "Sister Sister" if requested. In high school, she joined the show choir and a community theatre group, The Troubadours. After marrying the man of her dreams and moving from her hometown she sought out a different artistic outlet – writing.

To say that Renee is a romance addict would be an understatement. When she isn't chasing her kids around the house, working her day job, or writing, she jumps head first into a romance novel.